DATE DUE

FOLLETT

Crossing Montana

Crossing Montana

LAURA TORRES

HOLIDAY HOUSE / New York

Thanks to Carol Lynch Williams for unending
support and wisdom, Dean Hughes for
encouraging me at the beginning, and the true
friends who helped along the way: Rick, Cheri,
Laurel, Mette, Kim, Chris, John, Kurt, and Kevin.

Copyright © 2002 by Laura Torres
All Rights Reserved
Printed in the United States of America
www.holidayhouse.com

Library of Congress Cataloging-in-Publication Data
Torres, Laura.
Crossing Montana / Laura Torres.
p. cm.
Summary: While looking for her grandfather who is missing,
teenaged Callie examines her father's longtime absence
and its damaging effects on her family.

ISBN 0-8234-1643-7

[1. Family problems—Fiction. 2. Missing persons—Fiction.] I. Title.

PZ7.T64565 Cr 2002
[Fic]—dc21

2001059355

For Brennyn and Andrew

Crossing Montana

chapter one

"Callie, Grandpa's missing," Mom says, and holds the phone against her collarbone.

I look up from the *Seattle Times*. "Missing?" I swirl my Corn Flakes around the bowl with my spoon. "You mean he's on a fishing trip again?"

"*Missing.* Pack some clothes. We're going to Idaho." Mom puts the phone down and stares at me.

My stomach is clenched tight. I feel like I can't breathe. Hot acid burns in my chest.

I eat another spoonful of cereal. It tastes like paste.

"I don't want to go," I say. Not to mention my soccer game on Friday, the paper that's due, and my haircut appointment next week. "Grandpa will come back, just like always."

"We've *got* to go. Be there for Rachel, at least."

"How can us being there help?" Rachel is my grandmother, a solid-as-a-rock kind of person. I can't think of her needing help. It makes my heart beat fast and my palms sweat.

"He's always come back before."

I'm being difficult, but I can't stop myself.

"He took the truck this time. He's driving this time. What if he has an accident?"

Mom looks away from me, but her eyes well up and her nose twitches like it does before she starts to cry. Great. Now she's got me feeling guilty.

So I go to my room and start throwing clothes into my backpack. I change into sweatpants for the sixteen-hour drive and call my school to tell them I won't be there for a while. Actually, I tell them my daughter, Callie Gray, in the tenth grade, won't be in school due to a family emergency. Mom's voice is easy for me to do, but it feels like marbles are stuck in my throat. What a cruddy beginning to a school year. Mom starts hollering at Stinky Ronnie to get out of bed and start packing.

Then she shuffles around the house, which is a major disaster, putting a dish in the dishwasher, unloading a pile of laundry from the dryer, and going back to put something else in the dishwasher. Part of the reason the house is such a mess is because Mom cannot focus on one thing long enough to make a difference. The other part is because I don't have time to keep up the whole thing myself. I can stand a little clutter, but not dirty toilets, sinks, or showers. So I keep those clean, pick up when I have time, and push the vacuum around about once a week. While I clean, late at night, Mom sits and stares out the window, into the rain, or into nothing.

Mom's humming an Annie Lennox tune, which is what she always does when she's upset. Which means she's most likely thinking about my father. Really, she couldn't help thinking about him with Grandpa missing. Grandpa hasn't done this for two years, at least. I shove my paper and books off the bed and onto the floor, looking for a missing sock. I look under the bed and stand up too quickly. My head swims. I sit down on the bed for a minute. Probably just lack of sleep. I stayed up all night working on Biology homework, extra credit stuff I don't need. It was one of those nights where I slid into bed after 1:00 A.M., thinking I was tired enough to sleep this time. That the sound of the rain would put me to sleep. Wrong. Right at that floaty stage, not quite awake, not quite asleep, I'd freak myself out, wondering if that's what it felt like to die, and I'd have to relax and start all over again. I gave up about two-thirty, about the time the rain stopped, and turned on the light.

I find the sock, and try to concentrate on the one good thing about going to Idaho. Raphael Carmona. That thought makes my stomach feel sick, too, but in a good way.

I look in the mirror to see if I've changed since he's seen me last. Same blondish red hair, same green eyes, but straight teeth—I've gotten my braces off. He'll have to notice that. Maybe my cheeks have hollowed out just a little bit. I hope so, because I've always thought my face is too round.

There is some Pepto-Bismol in the kitchen cupboard and I go to get it. Stinky Ronnie's sitting at the table, slurping down a glass of orange juice.

"Where do you think Grandpa's gone, Callie?" he asks.

"Fishing," I say. All along I'm not thinking about Grandpa's being gone or Mom's paranoia about car accidents. Missing. I smile and tell Stink not to worry. I tell myself that history doesn't have to repeat itself.

chapter two

When we're ready to go, it starts raining again. We pack the car quickly, but our stuff gets wet. Why don't we have a garage like normal people? When you live in Seattle, you'd think you'd have a garage. I asked my mom about this once, and she said my dad, who'd designed our house himself, didn't want to waste space to store a car.

"He figured most people just fill their garages up with junk and end up parking the car out front anyway," she'd told me. "Besides, our lot is small, and your father wanted a garden. A big garden." She'd said this last part like it was a brilliant idea. Forget that it was never anything but an overgrown, weedy mess.

Mom has a bunch of stuff piled on the front seat of our old Mazda, so I'm forced to sit in the back with Stinky Ronnie.

"Move over, Stink," I say. His hair is bowl-cut, like

Moe, his favorite Stooge. Stink is obsessed with the Three Stooges. He came home one day from a friend's house with his hair cut that way, and Mom never even noticed until I pointed it out.

"Don't call me Stink," he whines.

"If the smell fits, wear it," I say.

"Knucklehead," he mutters.

I'm not sure why I feel like picking on him. He's not such a rotten kid, except for all his woo woo wooing and eye gouging routines, and he doesn't actually stink. It was his father who smelled bad. Like cigarettes and Old Spice and body odor all mixed together. I never liked Stan and he didn't like me, maybe because I reminded him my mother had been married before.

Stink sticks out his lower lip and narrows his eyes.

"Mom, tell her not to call me that."

When Ronnie was a newborn, Mom asked if I wanted to hold him. I was in first grade, but I remember it clear as anything. Mom tucked me into a corner of the couch and propped the sleeping baby up against my armpit. I put my face down into the fuzz on his head and sniffed, the way I'd seen Mom do it. He stunk like Stan. He'd been in the world only three days and he'd already absorbed everything I hated about my mom's new husband.

"Callie, how many times . . ." Mom stops rummaging through the glove box. "Where is the map? Callie?"

She pushes her curly bangs out of her eyes, and an unlit cigarette hangs from her lips. I guess she's forgotten it's there.

"How would I know?" I say. We've been on this trip a dozen times, but Mom is direction-impaired.

Stan left before Stink was even a year old, but the smell stuck around a long time, even after we'd stopped talking about him.

Once Mom finds her map and we get on the highway, I drift off into half-sleep pretty quick. I can fall asleep in the daytime, anytime, anywhere. It's only nighttime that gives me problems. So I'm not really listening to Mom. I'm thinking about Raf and hoping he doesn't have a girlfriend. I don't think so, because his e-mails come regularly, once every two weeks or so, and they're always signed "Love, Raf." When Mom starts to talk about an auction, I open my eyes.

"What kind of an auction?" I ask. I must be confused from sleeping.

"Haven't you been listening to me? Your grandpa and Rachel have decided to sell the farm, that's been certain for a long time. But the market's not good, and they've got debts to pay—they'll have to get rid of all the machinery. That I can see. But their personal belongings?" She's talking fast, with a catch in her voice. "They don't need to sell all that off, too. But Rachel says they want a fresh start—that they'll find a condo in town to live in."

She wipes at her eyes with the back of her arm.

"If that's what they want, then why are you so upset? That farm's too much work for them, anyway."

"I guess I just wish things would stay the same sometimes. Change isn't always a good thing, you know. There's something to be said for knowing what to count on in life."

She turns up the radio, so I don't answer. I doubt she was really talking to me, anyway. I get the feeling she talks to me for the same reason I talk to Stink. Because he's there.

She finally lights her cigarette and cracks the window open. Little splashes of rain land on the seat back and scatter droplets onto my lap. The smoke smell still comes in, though.

"I'm thirsty," Stink says.

Mom reaches underneath her seat and retrieves a juice box, which she hands Stink. He unwraps the straw, and tries to push it into the hole. I can see it coming. He's holding the box in the middle, all wrong.

"Stink . . . ," I begin. The straw goes into the box and juice squirts out all over my arm.

"You little dork!" I shout.

Mom turns around and looks at me.

"Callie Lucinda Gray!"

"Sorry," I say, quickly, not because I'm sorry but because I'm worried she's not paying attention to the road, with all her crying and talking and being outraged because Stink is a dork.

Stink hands me a wadded-up Kleenex from his pocket.

"Sorry, Callie," he says.

I stare out the window for a long time, wondering why Grandpa would leave without telling anyone where he was going this time. Was he upset about selling the house? Moving away from the farm? How do you run away from your problems? That I'd like to know.

I close my eyes and concentrate on the feel of the road.

"I can't drive anymore." Mom's voice wakes me up. We're pulled over on the side of the road. Stink is breathing heavily, asleep.

"You drive for a while, Callie." She hands me the keys and I push open the door. It feels good to stretch my legs. I've been driving for a year, since I was fourteen. I'm tall, five feet eight inches, and look a lot older than I am, so maybe that's why I never get pulled over. I'm also a good driver. Grandpa had me out driving a tractor as soon as I could see over the steering wheel.

Mom settles into the back and I take her place in the front seat. I've done this before, so it doesn't scare me.

"Remember, if a cop pulls you over, say your mother got carsick and you're just driving a few miles down the road to a gas station to call a relative. I'll moan and groan or something."

"I won't get pulled over," I say.

"Just take it easy."

She's not entirely comfortable with me at the wheel, even though it was her idea, because she doesn't fall asleep right away. She's always afraid we'll crash.

"Let me tell you a story," she says.

"About Dad?"

"Yes, about your dad. When you were just a toddler, maybe one and a half, Jack decided it was the best time for you to learn foreign languages. He saw a TV program on PBS, I think. Anyway, he hired a French tutor, a German tutor, and a Japanese lady that lived down the street to teach you."

Ça va? Oui, ça va bien, merci. Et toi? I wondered where I'd learned that. I had no idea I'd learned German and Japanese, too.

"So you started speaking German to the French tutor, French to the German tutor, and you never did get Japanese. Or at least Jack thought you didn't, because that Japanese neighbor didn't speak any English and wouldn't do anything but giggle at him."

Mom sounds happy, so I let her go on, even though I want to ask why he thought I should learn all three at once, or where he got money to pay for tutors. One thing I did know for sure, we never had any money.

"Jack had such big dreams. Such big hopes for you."

Oui, ça va. I must have been such a letdown.

"Of course he gave it up after a while," Mom says.

He gave it up, or did he give up on me? I push this thought away.

"He had big dreams." Mom sounds sleepy and I can see her eyes half-closed in the rearview mirror. "For you, Callie. He said you were really going to be something."

I'm holding the steering wheel too tight. The blood is draining from my hands and they start to tingle.

"What about the time he tried to teach me to swim?" I watch Mom in the rearview mirror. I know it's evil to bring this up, but I can't help it. I can't. She shifts in the seat and her eyes are wide open now. Her eyebrows squeeze together and lines form on her forehead and both sides of her mouth.

"That scared me," she says, barely a whisper.

chapter three

After a long silence, Mom finally goes to sleep. She doesn't believe I remember when Dad tried to teach me how to swim, but I do.

I have a theory that most people only *think* they can't remember when they were two or three years old. This is because their lives are constant and one memory runs into another and pretty soon you don't need to remember, say, Christmas when you were two, because Christmas when you are three and four are the same. Your mind just replaces one with the other. But when something—someone—is ripped out of your life, you remember.

My stomach feels heavy and I have an odd sensation I've forgotten something, but can't think what. I brought underwear, my toothbrush, dental floss.

The swimming pool memory is trying to invade my consciousness. My father's hands holding me around the ribs. Me in my new swimsuit. Green, with rows of pink ruffles on the butt. The strange, insecure feeling of being diaperless. The chlorine smell of the water in the pool fills up my nose and I want to sit on the edge and splash my feet.

What have I forgotten? Concentrate. I don't need to think about the pool. Toothpaste? Did I unplug the hair dryer? Lock the front door?

My father holds me above the water, his strong, trusted hands.

"Jack, I'm not sure about this," Mom says somewhere behind us.

There is a gap in the memory here. I don't remember him letting go. I try to stop the memory altogether. Lights. Did I turn off all the lights? The heater? Did I pack deodorant?

The cold water hits me and I suck in, but instead of air I gulp in water. I flail my arms and legs around, suck in again, gulp more of the nasty-tasting water. I try to cry, to breathe, to see my dad. Which way is out? Where are my dad's strong hands? Why doesn't he pick me up? Something is wrong. Something is very wrong. The world is going black. An arm wraps around my chest and pulls me out of the water.

Here, too, is a gap. Only my father's voice, much later.

"The only thing I can figure is she's too old. She's already lost what nature gave her to save herself in the water. We just waited too long, that's all."

Then me, wrapped up in a beach towel, eating a Popsicle.

I crank up the heat in the car and reach under the seat for a juice box, desperate to get the chlorine water taste out of my mouth that comes back to me every time I let the memory in. There isn't any juice. Leave it to Mom to pack one drink for three people on a sixteen-hour trip. I should have packed the food.

I still can't swim. Can't speak French or German or Japanese. Can't hardly get out of bed in the morning. Once in a while I let the darkness that comes with the morning cover me, just like I did when the swimming pool water covered my head.

Only there is no arm to wrap around me and pull me to the surface.

The cat. I forgot to leave food for the cat that's been coming to our back door. It's only a mangy stray, but it depends on me.

Stink wakes up when I pull the car off an exit and into a gas station to call Mrs. Houston, our neighbor, to ask her to take care of the cat.

"Are we there yet?"

"Not quite. Want a Coke or something?"

"*Soitenly!*" he says. Why can't I have a normal brother? "Can you get me Gatorade?" he asks.

"Anything for you," I say.

"Callie?"

"What now?"

"Why are you so mean sometimes and so nice other times?" He wipes some slobber off his face.

"I'm nuts, I guess." I go get some Gatorade and hope Mom doesn't wake up.

chapter four

We pull into Grandpa and Grandma's driveway at about midnight, stiff as plywood, tired and hungry. At least I'm tired. Mom and Stink slept on and off and I drove except the last few miles when Mom took over. Grandma meets us halfway to the door.

"My pumpkins!" Grandma hugs me and Stink, kissing our cheeks and foreheads.

"I'm not a pumpkin!" Stink says, but he's hugging her back, not minding the kisses.

"I've got fried chicken and some biscuits warm on the stove," Grandma says. My stomach growls even though we had burgers and shakes in Boise.

"That's really nice," says Mom. "But we can't eat a thing. We've been so worried."

"I'm hungry!" Stink yells. I could hug him myself.

"Of course you are!" Grandma seems relieved.

I watch Grandma fuss over the avocado green stove. She's wearing an apron that's got to be older than I am, tied around her waist, the strings barely long enough to make a knot around her ample figure. She's not fat, just solid. The kitchen looks exactly the same. Same old brown cupboards that could use a good scrubbing, a World's Best Grandma plaque on the wall I gave Grandma when I was five, and glass jars full of hard candies set all around. I try to imagine her in a brand-new condo, and decide she'll probably still wear the same apron and re-hang the plaque on the wall. It won't be so bad. The fried chicken smells wonderful and the sound of little spats of grease jumping from the pan makes my mouth water.

Stink is imitating Curly's headless chicken act, and Grandma is laughing. I guess it would be funny if I hadn't seen it a thousand times.

When we're all settled and eating around the table—even Mom's been talked into having a biscuit and milk—Grandma finally launches into it.

"I got up Tuesday morning and he wasn't here. His truck was gone and he didn't come home. I kept dinner warm until past the evening news. He never misses the news. Then I started calling everyone I could, everyone I could think of."

"Did you call the police?" Mom asks.

"Well, yes, on Wednesday," she says.

"And what did they say?"

"They say it looks like he meant to leave. He took some clothes and packed a lunch. His lunch bucket and the cooler are gone. Took his checkbook. They're not taking this too serious since he's always come back before. He's not even a missing person. I don't think they're looking for him."

"Did he leave a note or mention anything at all?"

"No. Nothing," Grandma says, and puts her head in her hands. "He used to at least leave a note. He would at least say he'd gone fishing, even if he didn't say where."

"Did you call Denny?" I ask. When Grandpa did this last time, it was his friend Denny who dropped him off in town, who saw him last. Grandpa gave the note to Denny to give to Grandma.

"He hasn't heard anything, either," Grandma says. "I hope there hasn't been an accident. . . ."

"This is just like when Jack left." Mom stops abruptly.

"Dad left to go on a trip across Montana," I say. "He planned it. We all knew about it." In our family, we don't talk about Dad leaving, so I jump on the opportunity. Maybe Mom wouldn't be so sad all the time if she'd talk about it.

"Yes, that's right," Grandma says. "It's nothing like what Jack did. We knew where he was."

"Callie, I don't think we should be talking about this. It's only going to upset everyone," Mom says. Her lips are drawn tight and I can tell she really, really wants me to shut up. But I know the reason they're all so worried about Grandpa is because of Dad. But it's not the same, it's not even close.

"Grandpa's coming back. There's no reason to think he won't." I'm trying to reason with them.

"Callie, stop," Mom says.

I'm getting a little upset now, but it doesn't stop me from taking another bite of my chicken. We never eat like this.

"What does Dad's trip have to do with Grandpa leaving, anyway?" It doesn't have anything to do with Grandpa leaving, but I want the conversation to keep going. Once the subject is closed, I need a crowbar to open it back up again.

The corners of Mom's mouth quiver and her hands are shaking a little bit.

Stink says, "Callie, just shut up. You're making everyone upset."

"You don't have anything to do with this," I tell him.

Mom's voice comes steady and angry. "Both of you get to bed right now."

"I've got your rooms made up in the basement," Grandma says.

Stink and I put our dishes in the sink and walk out of the kitchen, but I stop and listen at the door for a minute.

"What was his, you know, mental state?" Mom asks. "Was he drinking?"

"No, I don't think so. Hasn't said a word about selling the farm lately," Grandma says. "The day before he left, he sorted through some of his things and gave me a box of stuff for the auction. Just handed it to me, without a word."

I push the door open. "What about his fishing gear?"

Grandma and Mom look at me, surprised.

"What about it?" Mom says.

"Well, was it in the box of auction stuff?" I'm going to point out that if he kept some out, and it wasn't around the house, then of course he'd gone off fishing again, and that wouldn't be the end of the world.

"Yes, most of it, I think," Grandma says. "The stuff that didn't fit in the box, he put in the shed."

This hits me like a fist to my stomach. Grandpa would rather go without food or clothes than his fishing gear.

I head for the basement. Grandpa has a room there with a table set up with a vise for tying flies, and he keeps all his gear there, plus an antique bamboo rod, reels, float tubes, and a small boat. The bulletin board above his table is loaded with pictures of him with fish. There are even some of me, holding his catches.

I hold my breath as I open the door to the room. It's all gone. Only the bulletin board with all the pictures is still there, leaned up against a corner in the dark, unfinished room.

I let my breath go, but I still feel suffocated.

I nearly jump through my skin when someone taps me on the shoulder.

"Callie, I'm afraid to sleep down here. It gives me the creeps." It's Stink. "Can I sleep in your room? I'll stay on the floor. I'm more afraid to go back upstairs."

Stink is sniffling, his precursor to bawling. He cries way too much for a nine-year-old. It's like he's a baby stuck inside a fourth-grade body.

"Yeah, I guess." I don't blame him for not wanting to go back upstairs. We walk into the room where I've always slept. There is a single bed covered with old, matted stuffed animals and dolls with crocheted skirts. Grandma taught me how to crochet one year when we lived here for the summer, and I made skirts for all the dolls. I pick one doll up. Her hair is patchy and her plastic face is dirty. I tip her back and forth and her eyes open and shut. Stink makes himself a bed on the floor with another mattress he finds propped up inside the closet.

"But if you snore, I kick you out. And none of that Stooge stuff. Understand?"

"I understand," he says, suddenly all smiles.

I lie awake a long time, trying to push thoughts I can't think about Grandpa, and Dad, aside. The only one I entertain at all is why me and Mom and Grandma weren't reason enough to stay.

chapter five

The next morning, the distant noise of dirt bikes wakes me up. My stomach flips. It's Raf and his brother.

I fling back the covers, spilling the ancient mint green quilt bedspread on the bright pink carpet, and head for the shower. I've got to hurry, get outside, and pretend I just happen to have something to do. I rehearse acting surprised.

My hair won't do anything right and I've put on too much makeup. No one wears this much makeup for an early-morning chore down by the spud cellars. Also, I'm disgusted with myself that I didn't bring jeans and T-shirts, the kind of stuff you wear around a farm. I only brought my school clothes, which are nearly all black, either that or brown, and accentuate how skinny I am. I wonder if Raf will think I'm too thin. I brought my Wonderbra, but there's only so much you can do with a frame like mine. I wash everything off my face but the mascara and throw on an old baseball cap I find in the basement. Better.

"Good morning, pumpkin," Grandma says. "Want some fried eggs?"

"I'm going for a walk," I say. "Maybe later."

Grandma can see right through me. Her fried eggs are my favorite, done up in bacon grease with lots of pepper. I wouldn't be so thin if there were actual food at our house. Once in a while I cook a meal for Mom, Stink, and me, but mostly it's Taco Bell and Japanese fast-food, which I pick up after school with money I take from Mom's wallet. In the evenings we eat popcorn and drink Coke while Stink watches his Three Stooges videos for the ninety-thousandth time; Mom sits, smokes, and looks out the window, and I study.

"Ah. Raphael is out, isn't he? Don't worry. I told him you were coming. He'll be around. Now, how about some eggs?" Grandma holds up her spatula expectantly. I want to go outside, but more than that, I don't want to disappoint her.

"All right. I'll go for my walk later," I say and take a seat. The dirtbike sounds are closer now.

I've been in love with Raf before he even knew what a girl was. I remember the exact moment I knew I loved him. Grandpa had taken us both fishing, like he did every summer because, he said, Raf and I were dyed-in-the-wool fly fishermen. He said he could tell both of us had natural talent.

It was the summer I was eleven, and Raf was barely twelve. We spent the day mostly in comfortable silence, the sun beating down on us, but a gentle breeze taking the heat off. Even the water felt mild, not ice-cold like normal. We sat on the warm rocks on the riverbank for a break. Grandpa gave me half of his beer, which tasted disgusting, but I drank it anyway, hoping Raf wouldn't think I couldn't be one of the guys. Every boy I talked to about fishing back in Seattle gave me a hard time about it. They thought I was weird the way I went on and on about leader and flies and casting and what I'd caught. But Raf was different. We talked for hours, tied flies when Grandpa let us use his vise, and dreamed about the perfect fishing hole. He never thought it was strange that a girl could love fishing so much.

When I passed the beer to Raf for a drink, he turned it down and drank his seltzer water instead. I was a little embarrassed, but at the same time, as I watched Raf sitting there on the rocks, in his tank top and long shorts, face turned up to the sun and eyes closed, I knew I didn't want him to think I was just one of the guys anymore. I loved Raf, even if I couldn't put a label on it back then.

But last year, when we spent Christmas break in

Idaho, everything changed. Raf invited me to a party that a friend of his was having. Mom didn't want me to go, but Grandma convinced her it was okay.

"The Carmonas are nice people," she said.

"We don't really know them, do we?" Mom said.

"Mom, you don't care who I hang out with at school. You don't know any of my friends. I go to parties all the time where there is no one you know," I said, trying to keep my calm. Raf had finally noticed me and I wasn't going to let Mom's posing as a concerned mother stop me.

"Besides, I've spent entire summers with him! Who do you think I've been hanging out with all this time?" Wrong thing to say. Mom's eyes widened and her mouth pursed into a little O.

"We know Raphael and his family as well as anyone," Grandma said. "His grandparents used to live in the sugar company trailers, right across the street here. They came as seasonal farm labor, you know, a long time before Jack was even born. Other farmers had a hard time with their help—stealing and drinking—but those Carmonas were always hardworking and honest. I was happy for them when they finally got a place of their own."

Mom looked at me long and hard. It was all I could do not to roll my eyes at her.

I think how different Raf's family is from my own. A big family, and they all laugh together and hug and go on family vacations to Disneyland and Yosemite.

"None of those kissing games," Mom warned me, and I was out the door.

Kissing games is exactly what the party turned into. Spin the Bottle, to be exact, and Raf made sure the bottle pointed at me on his turn. We went into the dark closet together. I thought I was going to faint. I'd wished and wished and wished Raf would be attracted to me, and now I was petrified. I didn't know how to act, what to do, or what Raf was going to do. All of a sudden I was too nervous for anything to happen, but I knew I'd be disappointed afterward if it didn't. I wanted Raf to like me the way I liked him. All vacation I'd taken every opportunity to be alone with him, even turned my face toward his when we sat close together so he could kiss me if he wanted to.

He put his hands on my shoulders.

"Look, Callie," he said. "I like you a lot. . . . You don't have to worry about me trying to talk you into anything."

Talk *me* into anything? If I had an ounce of courage I would be trying to talk *him* into something.

"Not that I wouldn't want to. I would," he continued.

I forgot about being nervous.

"You mean you can't even kiss me?" I blurted out. I knew Raf and his family were Mormon, but I didn't really know what that meant, besides not drinking and smoking.

He laughed. "I can kiss you."

His lips met mine a little off-center. They were warm and soft and Raf smelled like fresh-cut grass. It was a long kiss, a kiss that still sends shivers up my spine. It took me a minute, after it ended, to become deeply embarrassed that Raf thought maybe I was expecting something more than that kiss. I couldn't sleep later that night, torn between wanting more from Raf and being embarrassed that he thought I wanted more. What kind of a boy felt like he needed to explain things right away, before we'd even kissed? I decided, long after I returned home, that Raf was exactly the kind of person I wanted in my life.

I'm still thinking about that kiss when Grandma brings my breakfast over to the table. Even though I'm still full from last night's feast, I dig in. I take a bite of the heavenly eggs and wash them down with a long drink of orange juice.

I pick up my breakfast and move to the family room, where I can see Raf and his brother Carlos riding their dirt bikes across the street near the spud cellars. A curtain of dust hangs by the side of the road, getting thicker as they continue to ride up and down the road and up and over the cellars, so all I can make out are their silhouettes. When we were younger, Raf, Stink, Carlos, and I used to play in those spud cellars, trying to scare the living daylights out of one another. They were creepy—dark and humid and the smell of dirt so thick it seemed hard to breathe.

I wonder if Raf is hoping to see me. What if he has a girlfriend? What if he doesn't like me anymore? What if he's forgotten me altogether? I'm nervous every time I see him. The e-mails are great, but real life is something different. If I lived here all the time, I'm sure we'd feel comfortable together and he'd be like a real boyfriend. I crave that comfort level with Raf. I'm tired of the butterflies and flip-flopping stomach and sweaty palms and not being able to make my mouth say what I want it to whenever I'm around him. Sometimes I miss the days when we were friends, before I loved him, because it was so much easier.

Even though I'd always loved it at Raf's house, I remember the first time I really *noticed* how things were there. I sat at the table eating cookies that Mrs. Carmona had just baked. There were little kids running around the house, nieces and nephews and neighbor kids, and Mrs. Carmona was offering everyone cookies. But the place was spotless. A chore chart hung on the refrigerator, along with a scattering of crayon pictures and pieces of Raf's homework with gold stars on them.

"My mom's way too strict," Raf told me that same day when she wouldn't let him come out late to get a soda with me and Grandpa. "She's driving me crazy!" I couldn't believe anyone would say anything like that about Mrs. Carmona. I thought I'd take fresh-baked cookies and someone who was proud of my gold star homework over staying up late any day.

When I finally get outside, the dirt bikes are far away. It's a little bit chilly, but I don't want to go back inside just yet. Instead, I head for the shed where Grandma said Grandpa put his fishing gear for the auction.

I pull the rusted latch open on the decaying door. Inside, it smells like mold and old paint and rotting wood. The streak of light I've let in shines on cobwebs and unidentifiable, rusted farm tools in the back.

With the door propped wide open, there is enough light for me to see Grandpa's things stashed along the wall on one side. I pull out his vest and feel a rush of sadness that Grandpa is gone. He'll be back, I tell myself, just like before. When I look at it closer, though, I see that it's stripped of everything personal. There are no flies attached to the pocket flap, no tiny containers of weights, hooks, or wax.

Next, I open his tackle box and examine all the different kinds of flies, each in its own compartment. There must be over a thousand flies. I pick up a blue-winged olive, in a compartment by itself in between two empty compartments. Strange that there's only one. Grandpa used to tie them by the dozens. How many hours did Grandpa spend tying each fly to make it perfect, like this one? I lift out the main compartment tray and underneath are all of Grandpa's fly-tying supplies. Bags of feathers and fur and different colored threads. Tiny iridescent beads and hooks of all sizes. A hackle that I know is worth close to a hundred bucks.

I try to imagine why Grandpa would auction off his gear. He couldn't possibly get enough money for it to make it hurt any less.

I think I hear the dirt bikes getting closer, so I put Grandpa's stuff away. I listen hard, but it was just my imagination. On a whim, I pick up one of Grandpa's rods and reel and step out into the backyard to practice casting. The rod feels too big and clumsy in my hands, so I go back to trade it for a smaller size. That's when I remember the bamboo rod.

There are only three rods in the shed and Grandpa has four. The three that are here are the only ones Grandpa uses. The fourth is an antique bamboo one that Grandpa's father bought in New York in the late 1920s. When I asked Grandpa about it once, he said it was too valuable to use.

"Someday I'll fish it," he always said. So where was it now? If Grandpa was trying to make money off his gear, wouldn't that rod bring in the most?

Unsettled, I close the shed door and latch it tight. I'm thinking about Grandpa's bamboo rod when I hear footsteps behind me. I turn around. Raf.

"Hello there," he says.

"Hi," I say, and think I'm going to faint. He's so beautiful. It's funny to talk about a boy being beautiful, but there's no other word to describe Raf.

"Rachel said you were coming," he says.

"Yeah," I say. Brilliant. I wish I could think of something charming to say, but looking at him is like looking into the sun. It almost hurts.

His black hair is shorter than the last time I saw him, tight on the sides and longer on the top, where the ends betray a natural curl. He looks a lot like James Dean, who I saw in an old movie once, except better. Raf is stronger-looking, and I'll bet taller, too. I wonder if I'm so attracted to him because we are opposites. I envy his deep, golden, smooth skin that tans so easily compared to my pale, freckled, sensitive skin that burns in no time flat.

"Sorry about your Grandpa," he says.

"His bamboo rod is missing, too," I say.

"The antique?" Raf asks. I nod my head.

We stand there for a minute, grinning at each other, despite what we were talking about. So he hasn't forgotten. I hope he notices that my braces are gone and that my face is thinner.

Just when the silence starts to get awkward, he moves close to me and kisses me lightly on the cheek. There is stubble on his chin and upper lip that wasn't there before.

"I missed you," he says, staying close. He is covered with dust, but he still has that clean grass smell. I wonder how he can be so cool and calm. My knees are nearly buckling and I can't think of anything to say. I go through this every time we see each other.

Grandma saves me.

"Callie! Raphael! Come on inside, *The Price Is Right* is on!" She slides the back door wide open and disappears. Raf and I look at each other, laugh, and head in. Grandma never misses *The Price Is Right,* and she loves to have an audience watch her win all the games, even when the contestants on the TV don't.

Grandma is playing the Lucky Seven game to win a Buick Regal and has only lost a dollar. The contestant has lost five. Raf sits down next to me, close, and we join in guessing the last two numbers. Grandma gets both of them. The contestant loses.

"You only need one dollar left to buy the car," Grandma says. "I would have had six!" Raf is so close to me that the hairs on his arm tickle against my own arm.

I think of Grandma on TV with Bob Barker, trying to win her Buick, and it makes my guts want to turn inside out. Grandma doesn't have good luck in real life. Raf takes my hand and squeezes it tight. His hand is warm and dry and I glance down at the smoothness of the back of it. I curl my fingers around his. My stomach flips. If only Grandma could have some luck. How can she stand to watch all these other people winning and losing?

"One dollar for a Buick and five left over to spare," Grandma says and shakes her head. "What do you think about that?"

"I think you're amazing," Raf says, but he's looking at me. Grandma gives me a smiling, raised-eyebrow look when she sees that Raf is holding my hand.

Mom stumbles in. She's wearing her bathrobe and her hair is sticking up all over. It takes her a minute to focus.

"Oh," she says when she sees Raf. She runs a hand over her hair and closes up her robe tighter, and takes the unlit cigarette out of her mouth. Raf's grip on my hand loosens.

"Callie, why don't you tell your friend here that it's not a good time," she says. I want the sofa to open up and swallow me. Then Raf is on his feet.

"It's all right," Grandma tells her. "Raphael knows what's going on."

"I'm sure he'll understand it's a *family* crisis," Mom says. She's smiling, trying to act all sweet, despite what she's saying. Acid burns in my throat.

Raf turns around. "See you later," he says.

"Bye," I say, but think *I'm sorry, I'm sorry, I'm sorry*.

This would never happen at Raf's house. It's the kind of place where you immediately feel comfortable, no matter what's going on. Mrs. Carmona looks just the way you would want your mother to look. She has a kind face with dimples and a wide smile. She would never, ever be so rude.

When Raf is gone, Mom turns off the TV. I try to let my anger at the way she treated Raf go. What's the use? It's miserable enough already without Mom and me fighting. We'd argue, Mom would cry, I'd feel guilty and end up apologizing. I know the routine. And this time, I don't want to apologize. She sits down on the couch and finds a pad of paper and pen on the coffee table.

"Now, then," she says. "We need to figure out a few things here. Let's make a list."

An alien may as well have landed in the middle of the living room. A list?

Grandma and I stare at her.

"Come on, let's think," she says, shifting uncomfortably. "Nothing's going to get done unless we get organized."

"What kind of a list?" I ask.

"I don't know, just a list of what we need to do," she says. "Rachel, don't you think we need a list?" Her lower lip quivers.

"If you think so," Grandma says.

"Yes, I most definitely think so," Mom says. "Now, what should we put on the list? Rachel?"

"Well, how about things for the auction," she says.

Mom brightens a little and her lip stops quivering. "Okay, there's a start," she says. She writes on the pad. "Callie? Any ideas?"

"How about ten more ways to ruin my life," I say. I get up and walk out the door, leaving Mom with her list.

I spend the rest of the day napping and tinkering with Grandpa's fishing gear out in the shed. I wonder what kind of flies were in the two empty compartments on each side of the blue-winged olive. I wonder where the bamboo rod went. I wonder if I can put the puzzle together. I wonder if Raf will come back to see me. I wonder if Mrs. Carmona would adopt me.

chapter six

That evening, I'm feeling tired, but having a hard time sleeping anyway in Grandma's basement. Every time someone flushes a toilet it sounds like the ceiling above my head is caving in and a waterfall lets loose through the exposed pipes on the wall. Grandma's and Mom's footsteps keep me awake, too. They are in the kitchen, I imagine, getting up and down for coffee and pacing while they worry.

They settle down after a while. Mom must have gone to bed, and the *creak, creak* of Grandma's rocker is constant. I finally drift off, the creak-creaking never leaving my consciousness.

I wake up, knowing I won't be going back to sleep again. I turn on a light and try to find a book to read.

Stink says something I recognize from a Stooge video.

He's talking in his sleep. Not only does he watch the Stooges all evening long, he quotes them in his sleep.

I grab some blankets and a pillow and make myself a bed on the recliner chair in the rec room. I settle down to read in the stillness of the house. The minutes go by like hours and the words blur on the page. I read the same sentences over and over without making any sense of them.

Mom and Grandma think I can't sleep because I don't want to sleep. They say it's psychosomatic. They've even got Stink believing I somehow do this to myself. But Grandpa believes me. I think about one time, maybe three years ago, but it seems like it was just last night.

It must have been daybreak, and I had drifted off for the first time that night over my book. Grandpa's booming voice startled me.

"How the hell are you going to help dig the tractor out of the shit if you ain't slept all night?"

That was his idea of being funny.

"You don't have a sympathetic bone in your body," I said.

He bent down and pressed his hand on my forehead. His hand was calloused and felt dry and rough against my skin.

"You ain't got a fever."

"I know. It's this sleeping thing. Like always," I mumbled. "Nobody believes me that I can't help it."

"Well, as long as it ain't just an act to get out of shit diggin'," he said.

"I wish." A few tears squeezed out of my eyes. I brushed them away, embarrassed.

He smiled at me and pulled the blanket up to my chin.

"You'll be good to go tomorrow."

"I know, Grandpa. Always am."

I'm thinking about Grandpa now, wondering if he's on a drinking binge. But I doubt it, because he's never taken his truck before. He hates drunk drivers worse than anything. Once in a while, when things have gone wrong, Grandpa overdoes it on the liquor and gets falling-down drunk. He disappears, then comes back, all apologetic. He's been picked up by the cops in town a few times, who return him home instead of taking him to jail. They know Grandpa and know he doesn't generally cause problems. But once, after Dad's trip, Grandpa went on a binge that lasted several days and when he didn't show up, Grandma got scared and called the cops herself. I only know this because I overheard Mom talking about it on the phone with Grandma a while back.

"Callie?" It's Stink.

"What are you doing out of bed?"

"I wasn't in the bed, I was on the floor," he says. "What's going on?"

"Just reading a book."

"No, I mean with Grandpa. What's going on? Why did he leave?"

"I don't know. Nobody knows. That's why we're here," I say. "Please, Stink, go back to sleep. This doesn't concern you." He is only a kid, after all.

"That's what everybody says. But I'm worried about Grandpa, too."

I try not to talk.

"Your dad left, my dad left, and now Grandpa," he says.

I hadn't considered the impact of this whole thing on Stink. Grandma and Grandpa treat Stink like their own grandson, since he never knew Stan, let alone Stan's parents. It's like Stan never existed. To listen to this family, you'd think Stink dropped from the sky.

"My dad was a different situation," I say.

"Yeah, tell me about it," Stink says. "Mom never cries for my dad. Only Jack. And now Grandpa."

I rub my forehead and will myself to feel drowsy.

"I want you to know I don't think you make yourself stay awake on purpose," he says. "In case you haven't noticed, I can't sleep, either."

"Yay for you," I say, but I smile. Sometimes the kid surprises me.

chapter seven

In the mornings, southern Idaho has a particular smell and feel to it. The land is flat and there is nothing to block the view of the horizon except a few shiny silver crop silos. The wind blows constantly and whips up a fresh dirt scent. I get a kind of reverse claustrophobia when we stay here. Too much wide-open space and you can see for miles and miles without really seeing anything.

I'm outside with the idea that I'm helping Grandma sort through her things for the auction. She and Mom had gotten up early and emptied the kitchen onto the picnic table and blankets laid on the grass. Mom's sitting inside, now, staring out the window.

I'm shaky from being up all night, but it feels good that it's daylight and I can take a nap later.

"What about this?" I ask, holding up a small pitcher of heavy, ruby red glass.

Grandma looks at it for a long moment.

"Put it in the box."

The box, actually several huge boxes, is where the stuff to be sold off goes.

I set it gently inside, next to a Big Boy cookie jar.

Grandma is carefully stacking her china in a bubble wrap–lined box. It's not really china; in fact it's heavy stoneware, but it's the best she's got and so she's always called it her china.

Another thing about this place, it's so quiet it makes me uncomfortable. No traffic noise, no neighbor kids, no stereos. Even the wind is near silent, with not much but dust to blow up this time of year. During the summer, I used to like to climb up on Grandma's roof and stare out at the fields of canola a short distance off. Canola crops are the brightest yellow you can imagine, brighter than mustard. The wind would blow patterns in the fields of yellow so it would look like a golden ocean. But now a lot of the farmers have gone back to growing potatoes or sugar beets. Grandma says prices for both are down and they'll all take a loss this year, though.

"Look how high I am, Callie," Stink shouts. He's on the swing.

I concentrate on the rhythmic whooshing. The swing is made out of bright yellow rope tied around the top of the steel frame, with a wood plank for a seat. The plank digs into the back of your thighs and makes your butt hurt for two days afterward, but it's the closest to flying you can get.

The next dish I pick up is a clear blue plate. It's old, judging from how much it's scratched up. I think I should make some decisions on my own, because it doesn't seem efficient for me to ask Grandma about every little thing. In the box it goes.

Then I pick up a small ceramic bowl with an ugly orange and red design on it. In the box.

"Wait."

Grandma's hand on my arm startles me.

"I'm keeping that."

I hand her the bowl.

"Jack made that in the sixth grade," she says. "He was gifted at art, a genius. Could have been real success-ful as an artist."

I stare at the bowl and try to see the genius in it. It's hideous.

"Why didn't he stick with it?" I ask. Of all the jobs my dad tried, I don't remember any involving art. Except maybe the job with the kids' software company. Dad referred to it as being creative, but I don't know exactly what it was he did.

"Jack was so good at so many things, he never seemed to want to do just one," she says.

She puts the bowl on the back steps, with the small pile of other dishes she's decided are necessities. She has a look on her face that makes me want to keep my mouth shut. Her mind is already spinning with thoughts of my dad. I go back to sorting dishes, careful to save anything that looks handmade with an ugly design on it.

I remember Dad on one of those days when he had his bedroom door shut and I'd have to eat lunch out of the cereal box.

The phone rang. "Hello?"

"Is Jack Gray home?" a man's voice asked.

"He's sleeping in his room," I said.

"Is he sick?"

"I don't think so, he just doesn't want to get out of bed again," I said.

The man on the other end didn't say anything.

"Hello?" I'd asked again.

"Yes, I'm here. Would you please wake your daddy up and tell him Mr. Walton is on the phone?"

"Okay," I said, but it wasn't going to be easy.

I put the phone down in the kitchen and opened the bedroom door a crack, even though I wasn't supposed to. The radio was on real low and he had his face to the wall, so I couldn't see if he was awake or not.

"Daddy . . . Are you awake, Daddy?" No answer. I walked over and tapped him on the shoulder.

"What?" His voice was sharp. He turned over, his eyes wide open. So he wasn't sleeping.

"Daddy, Mr. Walton is on the phone," I said. "He said I should wake you up. I'm sorry."

"Tell him I'm sick and I can't come in today."

"I already told him you weren't sick, you were just sleeping. Should I tell him I made a mistake?" I felt bad for not realizing I should have lied.

Dad stared at the ceiling for a while, until I thought maybe Mr. Walton would get tired of waiting. But when he finally got out of bed and went to the phone, Mr. Walton was still there. They talked low so I couldn't hear from where I sat outside the bedroom door.

I had wished I was a better liar. Maybe he would have kept that job. I shake the memory from my head.

A stack of white plates looks fairly new and I ask Grandma if she wants to keep them.

"I would, but we ought to put them in the auction. They'll bring in a few dollars," she says.

With no warning, my insides start to hurt, my head feels heavy, and my eyes sting. I can't cry, I think. There's been enough crying to go all around a hundred times. These things out here are just a bunch of crappy dishes, not babies or something. I take a deep breath. My teeth feel like they're coated with dust.

The dull thud of Stink hitting the ground is followed by screaming. Mom's.

She runs out the sliding-glass door and past me and Grandma before we even have a chance to react.

The only noise is still coming from Mom.

When I get to where Stink's fallen off the swing, he's lying on his back, his eyes wide and his mouth opening and shutting like a fish.

"Speak to me, Ronnie! Ronnie! Say something!" Mom is randomly pounding on his chest.

"He's got the wind knocked out of him," I say.

"Rachel, call an ambulance!" Mom shrieks. Grandma starts back to the house.

"Wait, just wait," I say. I push Stink's feet up so his knees go to his chest. He takes a breath and starts to bawl.

"Ronnie!" Mom is still screaming and pounding.

I grab her hands to stop her from beating him to death. Grandma has come back and is helping Ronnie to his feet. She brushes the dust and grass from his shirt and pants.

"Darn swing," she mumbles. "I told your grandpa it's nothing but a death trap."

"Where in the hell is Grandpa? He should be here taking care of things!" Mom is still shrieking.

I decide not to mention that Grandpa would be either out in the fields or in town this time of day. Or that I've fallen off this very swing at least twenty-two times.

Grandma shakes her head and puts her arm tightly around Ronnie. He stops crying.

"The Lord giveth and the Lord taketh away," she says.

I bite my tongue to keep from saying the Lord didn't take Grandpa anywhere. The evidence suggests he drove his truck. Himself. And packed a lunch. And maybe, just maybe, he's got the bamboo fishing rod with him.

And then it comes to me. It's September. The Baetis hatch on the Gallatin River. The nymphs on the bottom of the river rise to the top, transformed into winged insects. Perfect fly-fishing conditions. Grandpa once said to me, "Callie, one thing I'll do before I die is catch the Baetis hatch on the Gallatin River." He went every year he could, and either missed it, or it was a bad year for the hatch. He gave up quite a while ago, as far as I knew. But that could be it. The Baetis hatch could be the answer.

After the three of them have gone back inside the house, I pick up the piece of plywood that launched Stink and fit the grooves back into the loop of rope. I can't stand the tension and the quiet and the unanswered questions that everyone's already got answered.

I pump my legs as hard as I can, not caring about the plank digging into my legs. I close my eyes and fly. I decide, right then and there, that I've got to do something. I can't stand this meltdown one more day. I'm going to find Grandpa and, more importantly, get out of this place.

The rest of the day flies by as I'm making plans, finding Grandpa's maps, the ones we'd marked on where we'd like to go, and stealing money out of Mom's and Grandma's wallets. I've got a few twenties and some change. I also go through all the drawers and cupboards where there might be dollars and change stashed. I even search the cushions of all the furniture and get eight dollars and forty-two cents. A bill sunk deep into the crevice of an orange velour couch in the basement turned out to be a five.

Stink is the only person I tell about my plans. Stupid, I know, but it bothers me more to be leaving him alone at night in the basement than to be leaving Mom or Grandma. They are so preoccupied, no one has even noticed Stink is alive. Except me. Because he snores at night. But I know what it's like to be a kid and have someone leave you without warning or explanation. I'm leaving a note for Mom, of course, but I can't trust her to share it with Stink.

"I'm leaving," I told him after breakfast, holding his shoulders tight and looking him straight in the eyes. "I'm going to find Grandpa and bring him back."

His eyes got big and his mouth dropped open.

"You know where he is?" he asked.

"I have an idea. You can't tell anyone. Do you understand?"

He nodded his head, but he was looking at the ground. I gave him a shake.

"Look at me!"

He sniffled and looked up.

"I'm leaving tonight. There will be a note for Mom and Grandma. But they can't know until after I'm gone."

"Why? If you know where he is they'll *want* you to bring him back. We could all go!"

Because I could be wrong, and because I can't bear the pressure of all this worrying one more day, and because I need to do this all by myself. And because I want to get away.

"Because Mom and Grandma need to take care of things around here. They, and you, need to stay in case Grandpa comes back" is what I told Stink.

"But if you know where he is . . ."

"Just trust me," I told him. "You've got to trust me."

He looked at me uncertainly, and I'm sure he was trying to figure out why I would tell him such a big secret. And what to make of it. But he surprised me.

"Okay, Callie," he said. "I'll trust you."

"Good. Now don't worry about sleeping alone. You can sleep in my bed, or I bet Mom would let you sleep on the couch upstairs," I said.

"I'll be all right," he said. "Raf said he'd take me for a ride on his dirt bike today."

"Wear a helmet, Stink. Tell Raf I said you have to."

It's impossible to sleep that night. Stink falls asleep right away on the floor next to my bed, but my eyes are wide open. Why are Mom and Grandma taking so long to go to bed? It's midnight and I can still hear their footsteps and Grandma's rocker.

I go over all my plans again. I've thought of everything, I think. I hope I'm right about where Grandpa's gone. If I'm not, I'll have a lot of explaining to do.

Finally, *finally*, the creaking and walking and toilet flushing stop and all is quiet upstairs. I force myself to wait another half hour, just to be sure.

I get out of bed and tiptoe to get my things. I'm already wearing my clothes—I went to bed with them on. I've got money, clothes, and even Mom's credit card for good measure packed in my backpack and an old duffel bag I found in the basement.

I sling the backpack over one shoulder and the duffel bag over the other. As I get to the bottom of the stairs, I trip and fall, sending the two bags crashing into the walls on either side of me.

"Shoot," I whisper, "shoot, shoot, shoot." My knee hurts bad and I have to take deep breaths to keep from shouting out. When the pain dies down a little, I hold my breath and listen to see if I've woken up Stink. He's not snoring, but there's no movement. I sit on the stairs for a minute, to be sure. Then I gather my things and head out to the car.

When I open the front door the cold night air hits my face. It surprises me how extreme the temperatures are here. You can sweat like a pig all day and at night the sweat will actually ice up on you.

The keys. I've forgotten to get the keys to the car. I set my bags on the front porch and go back inside. I leave the door open, propped with a rock because it's so squeaky.

I search through Mom's jacket pockets, her purse, everywhere I can think. It's been four or five minutes already and I'm getting frustrated. Think, think, think. The laundry. I find the keys in her jeans pocket in the hamper.

I practically run out to the car, slowing down only to carefully close the squeaky front door.

The doors of the car are unlocked and I slide in behind the wheel. My stomach is fluttery and I feel like someone will try to stop me any moment, so I hurry. I fumble with the keys and finally get the old car started. I back out of the driveway way too fast, hitting the slight ditch at the end hard. Whump! The car heaves up and down and something on the underside hits the dirt. I throw the car in drive and drive away. I keep the speed limit even though I want to gun it. There were no speed limits in Montana when Dad went on his trip. I wonder if he felt like he was flying. The gas gauge is on empty, but I drive as far away as I think I can go before I stop at an all-night gas station. The station has the quick-pay pumps, and I use Mom's credit card. So far, so good.

I'm on my way to West Yellowstone.

chapter eight

It feels strange to be out at night, let alone driving a car by myself. It's a little spooky, driving past all the fields, where the darkness goes on and on, barely broken up by the occasional farmhouse or silo. The spud cellars lie there like big sleeping monsters. And there are no streetlights like in the city. I can barely make out the road. Even though I don't sleep well, and I'm awake for at least a few hours in the middle of every night, I never go outside.

There were a few times when I was little, before I had sleeping problems, when Dad would come into my room and wake me up.

"Callie, you've got to come outside and see," he would say. "Come see what Daddy's found in the sky." It was rare to have a perfectly clear night in the Pacific Northwest, one that was clear and dark enough to see many stars, especially in the city.

I'd be freezing outside, thin pajamas and bare feet, but he would be so excited and happy I didn't dare complain or delay him for even a minute to put on something warm.

"Look up there, look up between the farthest two pine trees," he'd said once. "Do you see the three bright stars in a row? No, over there. That's right. Those three stars make the belt in Orion the hunter. Do you see?"

"I see, Daddy," I'd said, even though I wasn't sure I had the right three stars, and I sure didn't see anything that looked like a hunter, or a belt.

There was one night when Dad even woke up Mom to come out and see. I looked up at the sky and it seemed fireworks had exploded, fanned out, and then frozen there. Streaks of different colors filled the night sky, pink and orange and everything iridescent.

"Those are the Northern Lights," Dad said. "A rare thing, this far south. I think we ought to move north, as far north in Canada as we can go just so we can see the Northern Lights."

"But we're seeing them here," I protested. I didn't want to move to Canada. You never could tell when Dad meant what he said.

"I'm going to look into it tomorrow," Dad said. "Wouldn't you like to live in Canada?" he asked Mom.

"Do you think you could keep a job there?" Mom asked.

Next thing I knew, I was hustled into bed and listened to Mom and Dad argue until I fell asleep.

The next day Dad said he couldn't get out of bed, something about it being too dark, and would I be a good girl and get myself some breakfast? We never did move to Canada.

Now, I wonder if you can see the Northern Lights in Montana. I wonder what Dad was after on that trip. I wonder if the darkness he had in him that wouldn't let him get out of bed in the morning is the same kind that I have.

I hear a funny bumping sound coming from the rear of the car. The radio is on loud, so I turn it down and listen. *Thump. Thump-thump.* I grip the steering wheel hard and all the blood drains from my face. Do I have a flat tire? The car seems to be cruising just fine. *Thump-thump-thump.* The sound is coming from the back left side of the car, so I know it's not an engine problem, but what? I'm feeling light-headed.

It must be something with the tire. I panic because I'm not sure if there's a spare or even if there are tools to change a tire. Not that I know how, anyway. I slow up the car, but the *thump-thump*ing gets faster and louder.

I turn on the emergency blinkers and turn off the engine. It is dead quiet. And eerie. No other cars on the road, nobody around but me. I notice for the first time how many stars are out, fading now in the first hint of daylight. I take the keys from the ignition and reach for the door.

Thump-thump-thump. I leap out of the car and run. I stop a few yards away and try to quell the adrenaline rushing through my body. Running away from the car on the shoulder of a highway in the dark isn't going to do me any good.

Okay, think. The car is stopped. It's not the tire. The engine is off. It's not the engine. Then what? I practically tiptoe back to the car. My heart is trying to beat its way out of my chest.

Thump-thump. Then a tiny, faraway-sounding voice. From the trunk. I feel like I'm an actress in a really bad horror flick. Don't go near the car! Run away! Don't open the trunk! I can hear the audience screaming.

The voice and thumping get louder as I get close.

"Callie? Callie! Let me out! Callie?!?"

I jam my keys into the lock and throw open the trunk. I put both my hands around Stink's neck, ready to throttle him. He screams.

"What are you doing? What are you doing? You idiot!" The words tumble out and I am shaking. Stink pries my fingers from his neck and scrambles out of the trunk.

"I thought . . ." He tries to catch his breath. "I

thought I could unlatch the backseat. You know, like when Mom lays the backseat flat if we've got something big in the trunk—"

"What were you thinking?" I scream at him again.

"There's no latch from the trunk side," he offers. "I got scared. I wasn't sure how long my air would last."

"A lot longer than it's going to last now!"

Stink puts his hands to his throat and backs away from me.

"What were you doing in the trunk?"

A truck roars by, whipping up litter and dust.

"I wanted to come with you. Raf said it was danger-ous for a girl to be traveling by herself—"

"You told Raf about this?" I'm so angry I feel like the world is spinning around me.

Stink is seriously scared of me by now and looks like he wants to bawl.

"It just slipped out," Stink says. "I didn't mean to. I didn't tell Mom or Grandma. Raf was worried. He said you shouldn't go. I thought if I came, too . . ."

I get right in Stink's face and push my finger into his chest.

"How, just how, Mr. Wizard, is having a nine-year-old brother who still wets the bed and is afraid of the Chuck E. Cheese puppets going to help?" This is mean, but I'm still stark-crazy mad.

So he bawls. I stare at him a long, long time, pressing my finger harder until he gives and backs up. I walk over to the passenger side of the car.

"Get in."

"What?" he says.

"I said, get in. We've got to get going."

"I can come?" he asks. "I brought extra clothes and a toothbrush."

"Well, I'm not leaving you here, and I'm certainly not turning around," I say. It's getting lighter by the minute. I curse the farm life that forces everyone to get up at the crack of dawn. No way could we make it back before Mom and Grandma were up and already hysterical. The plan is not to come back without Grandpa, and I'm sticking to it.

We drive for an hour without speaking. I'm still trying to calm my insides down. It's not that I couldn't find Grandpa with Stink along. I begin to doubt if this trip was even about Grandpa at all. Stink has stopped crying and is sucking in the little hiccups he gets afterward. I can tell he's trying really hard not to bug me. I look over at him when I think he's asleep, but he's just staring straight ahead.

"I don't wet the bed anymore," he says.

"I know."

"And I'm not afraid of big, dopey puppets."

I laugh. What else can I do?

chapter nine

That afternoon, Stink and I eat lunch at a sandwich joint in Island Park, the last town before the Montana border. We split the cheapest thing on the menu, grilled cheese, and drink only water, because I'm concerned about our money supply. I hadn't counted on Stink.

When we're done, I make him wait in the car while I use the pay phone. I have to call information first, which takes a whole dollar, to get Raf's number.

"Hello?" It's Raf. Thank goodness.

"Raf, it's Callie."

"Where are you? Ronnie said you were going to leave—" He talks fast, but I cut him off.

"Look, Raf, I didn't want Stink to tell anyone. I think I know where Grandpa might be. His bamboo rod is missing, he's taken a bunch of flies with him, bluewinged olives, so it only makes sense. . . ." I try to explain.

"Callie, why did you go? Don't you know how worried everyone is? Your mom came over today, ready to kill me or something," he says. "I tried to tell her I didn't know where you went. But I did tell her Ronnie is with you. He is, isn't he?"

"Yeah, he stowed away. I'm sorry, Raf. I'm sorry Mom thinks you're involved. She's a little uncomfortable about me and you."

"Obviously," Raf says, and then we're both quiet. I'm not even quite sure why I've called him. But just the sound of his voice is reassuring, even if his words aren't.

"I need to do this by myself because I might be wrong," I finally say. "But I don't think I am, and I don't intend to come back without Grandpa. If I had to drag around Grandma and Mom and Stink . . . well, I am dragging around Stink and it's bad enough. Raf, they're hysterical."

"Well, when you consider your dad's, you know, accident . . . ," Raf says.

"There's no reason to think Grandpa's been in an accident like Dad."

"But I thought . . . ," Raf says.

"You thought what?"

"Nothing. I'm just worried about you." Raf's voice is gentle.

My scalp feels tingly and my face is hot.

Raf lets out a long breath.

"What I want to know is if you are all right," Raf says. I push thoughts of Dad away.

"Of course I'm all right. I haven't even been gone a whole day yet." I'm grateful for the change of subject.

"I miss you," Raf says.

"I miss you, too," I say, and my body actually aches this truth.

"I waited months to see you again, Callie, and then you up and leave on me a day later."

"I'm sorry. But I've got to get this worked out. If I don't, no one will," I say.

"I'm sorry, too. For you. About your family."

There is silence again.

"Callie? Will you call me if you need me?" Raf asks.

"Yes," I say, "but I'll be fine."

As I hang up the phone, I think about needing someone. I would like to need Grandpa. I would like to need Grandma and Mom. I needed my father. But I can't let myself need anyone anymore, because then what would happen? Who would take care of everything?

It isn't until Stink and I are driving around looking for fly-fishing shops that I start to think about Dad's accident. I've memorized the newspaper article and every detail of the photo that ran with it. *Fairview, Montana. A one-car accident claimed the life of a Seattle, Washington, man in the early-morning hours Tuesday. Jack Gray, 32, collided with a steel and wood sign at the Montana/North Dakota border. Emergency workers transported Gray to Memorial Hospital, where he was pronounced dead. Relatives say Gray, husband and father of one, was on a vacation, touring the state.*

The picture is of a tow truck getting ready to haul Dad's car from the accident site. He'd almost made it all the way across Montana. Just inches away from crossing the state line. Mom has the article stashed away in a box near the one with her high school and wedding mementos. It's in the box all by itself, like it's waiting for something else to fill the empty space.

I see a good-looking fly shop and pull into the parking lot. It's got a carved wood sign out front, and in the window is an advertisement for guide services. I don't trust a shop that doesn't have its own guides. I try to clear my mind and concentrate. I take the little box that contains the one blue-winged olive Grandpa left behind out of the glove compartment.

"Stay here," I tell Stink.

When I push the door open, a string of bells tied to the handle jingles, and a man with a baseball cap comes out of a back room.

"Can I help you?" he asks, grinning at me and raising his eyebrows high. I guess they don't get many fifteen-year-old girls in here.

"I hope so." I walk up to the counter, dump the fly into my palm, and hold it out to the man. "If you had an antique bamboo fly rod, and you were fishing these, where on the river around here would you go?"

He whistles, low, and looks at me like I've just asked him if he would dye my hair purple.

"There's lots of places you could go," he says.

"I forgot something," I tell him. "If you were an old man. With the antique rod and this fly. And you didn't bring waders with you."

The man looks at me long and careful.

"There are about a hundred places. But there was an old guy in here yesterday. Rented waders and a net," he finally says.

"What did he look like?" I ask. It could be Grandpa. I'm elated at finding a clue on the first try.

"Hmm . . . skinny guy, halfway bald . . ."

Grandpa's got a large build and hasn't lost too much of his hair, but it is thinning a little. I want to believe it's him. "Anything else?" I ask.

"He bought some flies," the man continues.

This is a blow. Grandpa would never fish with store-bought flies. But I'm not quite ready to give up.

"Which kind? Could you show me?"

The man walks around the counter and points to a cubby full of big, bright, fluffy flies with lots of feathers tied in. Only a bona fide novice would go for those.

"No, that wouldn't be Grandpa," I say. "Thanks for your help." He goes back behind the counter, and I walk quickly out of the store. I can tell the man is staring at my back as I leave.

"Well? Do you know where he is now? Can we go get him?" Stink asks. He's bouncing up and down on the seat.

"Don't be stupid," I say, mostly to myself. I rest my head on the steering wheel for a minute.

I visit the rest of the fly shops in town that afternoon. There are six. I don't have any solid leads, just a list of places on the Gallatin River that are particularly good fishing right now. I know that nobody gives away their best holes to any old person who walks in through the door, but at least it's a start.

We're getting low on gas, so I pull into a station, glad that it's another one of those quick-pay pumps. I don't want to face a clerk.

I stick the card in the slot and after a second it comes back out at me. Rejected. I stick it back in. Rejected again. The little screen on the pump says See Cashier. Great.

When I get inside, I hand the card to the cashier, a young woman, twenty or twenty-one. She's got long, fake fingernails painted bright red and frizzy long blond hair.

"The machine won't seem to take this card," I say.

"That machine is finicky. Wind must be blowing the wrong way," she says. I'm off the hook. But then she says, "Whose card is this? You aren't old enough."

"It's my mom's," I say. True enough. "She sent me to get gas for her."

The woman gives me a once-over and swipes the card in her machine.

"Hmm," she says, and tries it again. She taps her nails on the counter. I look out the window and see Stink with his face pressed up against the window.

"Sorry. It's been rejected," the woman says. "Tell your mom she better call her bank."

My face is burning hot, but I try to act cool.

"Okay, thanks, I'll tell her. Sorry for the trouble." My face is still hot when I leave, but it's because I'm mad at Mom. This is her only credit card, and she uses it all the time. Every time you use it, you get a percentage in bonus bucks to spend on a new GM car. Mom's never had a new car, and she talks about it all the time, even to grocery clerks, especially when they look at her funny for buying groceries on credit. She's only got 850 bonus bucks for her new GM car. She'll never be able to save enough to make a difference. The card must have gone over the limit when I stopped for gas last night.

"The card wouldn't work. We can't get gas," I tell Stink, who seems unconcerned.

"It's probably the magnetic strip," he says. "Mom

usually rubs it on her pants a few times before she uses it. She says it's because she uses it so much."

"Let's hope that's it," I say, and try to put it out of my mind. I go back in and pay cash for half a tank of gas.

I want to start looking for Grandpa on the river right away, but it is getting dark and Stink is complaining about being hungry.

We go to an all-you-can-eat buffet place where I buy a single dinner because of the money I had to spend on gas. There's a great big sign over the cash register that says No Sharing. I make Stink bend over and hold his stomach like he's sick.

"He's got a stomachache, so he won't be eating," I tell the clerk when she looks at us suspiciously.

"Why isn't he at home?" she asks.

"Because our parents are out of town," I say, "and there's no food in the house."

Stink lets out a moan.

"Are you sure he's all right? He looks bad," the clerk says.

"Oh, he gets this way all the time," I say. "It's a genetic thing." I smile, and kick Stink in the shins because he's moaning again.

"Ow!" He stands up straight. I hustle him to a table in the corner, far away from the clerk, and I fill my plate with food.

"Here you go, Mr. Drama," I say as I unload some of the food onto a stack of napkins in front of him.

"Hey, you said act sick," he says.

We go through four plates of food, which I fill as inconspicuously as I can. We're almost stuffed full when the clerk appears at our table, carrying a tray of desserts. Stink has got a mouthful of fried chicken, and he's holding the picked-clean leg bone in his hand. In front of him is a heap of crumbs.

I try to say something, but the words stick in my throat.

The clerk sets down two plates, one in front of me and one in front of Stink, with apple pie and a big scoop of vanilla ice cream on each.

"Thought you and your brother would like some dessert," she says.

"Thanks!" says Stink and digs in. The clerk smiles.

"Glad you're feeling better," she says, then gives me a look that I can't quite figure out. She glides away as quietly as she snuck up on us.

I feel completely humiliated and grateful at the same time. The pie tastes really good.

We drive around that night looking for the cheapest motel we can find, but it turns out most places are full. In every parking lot, I search for Grandpa's truck. He might be staying in a motel, but most often he parks his truck in a secluded spot and sleeps in the back in a sleeping bag. I finally settle on a grungy-looking motel that costs almost twice what I'd hoped to spend. So I ask for a single and make Stink hide in the car.

"You got a credit card?" the keeper barks at me.

"Yes," I say, trying to stay calm. He must think I'm older than I am. The extra makeup I've put on and my shoes with a small platform seem to make a difference. I've also got my hair pulled back from my face because I think it looks more sophisticated than straight down. Still, I was expecting him to ask where my parents were.

"But I'd rather pay cash, if that's okay." I'm too nervous to try and use Mom's credit card again.

"Pay in advance then," he says. He prints me out a receipt and I hand over the money. "Checkout's at 11:00 A.M."

"We're in luck," I tell Stink when I open the door to the room and see a green vinyl couch beside the bed.

"Who has to sleep on the couch?" Stink asks.

"One guess," I say. He plops down on the couch and sulks.

I throw him a blanket from the bed. The blanket doesn't seem all that clean, but what can I do?

"Hey, Callie, get this," Stink says. It's going to be a Stooge story. He knows every detail of each show, even the mistakes. "In one episode Moe and Curly throw a bucket of water on Larry. But later, when they throw the bucket away, you can see the bucket doesn't have a bottom!" He laughs hysterically and recites a little monologue.

"Go to sleep, Stink," I say. Then, mostly to myself, "We'll start looking tomorrow. With any luck, we'll be back at Grandma's tomorrow night." I cross my fingers and try to sleep.

chapter ten

We wake up early the next morning. Adrenaline rushes through my guts and I can't think clearly, except for the line from the Three Stooges Stink kept repeating, something about a porcupine and lots of nyuk nyuks. I want to go home. Back to Seattle. I want this never to have happened. I'm an idiot to think I could solve everything. What am I doing? I've only caused more trouble. I double over and try to stop the churning in my stomach and the heart palpitations that are making it hard to breathe. My palms are sweaty and my head feels light.

I remember Dad practicing breathing exercises in the morning. I had crawled into bed with him early one morning after Mom had left for work and lain across his chest. I remember his hand felt warm on my back. He pressed his hand hard into my back, almost too hard. He was inhaling deeply through his nose and exhaling through his mouth. His chest rose and fell, with me sandwiched between it and his hand. It was great fun until I turned my head to look at his face and saw that it was pinched tight and he had a wild look in his eyes.

"What are you doing, Daddy?" I asked.

"Breathing exercises," he answered, barely whispering.

"Why?" I asked. "Why, Daddy?"

His eyes were closed and he didn't answer. His chest went up and down.

After a few minutes he stopped breathing so hard and patted my back.

"Sometimes I have a hard time getting out of bed in the morning," he said. "The breathing seems to help. Let's go get you some breakfast."

Dad had been feeding me seaweed and tofu soup for breakfast after he found out that an Asian diet was supposed to be the most healthful, so I was surprised when he poured me a bowl of Froot Loops.

"Are you going to be all right, Daddy?"

"I think so," he said.

He spent the rest of the day in his room with the door closed, and only emerged right before Mom was supposed to get home. I ate the rest of the box of cereal for lunch. Even though I was used to Dad staying in bed, something in me felt uneasy that day.

Now, I lie back on the bed like he did that day, and breathe deeply. I try to empty my mind and distance myself from my physical pain. In and out. In and out. It's working, and I almost drift off to sleep again.

"I'm hungry," Stink says. "Can we get some breakfast?"

I roll out of bed and rifle through the duffel bag, and get two granola bars and an orange that I'd taken from Grandma's house.

"Breakfast is served," I say.

Stink wrinkles his nose at the granola bars while I peel the orange for both of us.

"Why don't you go get something else?" he asks.

"No money for it," I say.

"Oh."

I try not to feel bad, but I can't stop the churning in my stomach. When we finally drive into Montana, I feel a little better.

The Baetis hatch doesn't happen until after lunch, so we spend the morning walking around West Yellowstone. I keep my eyes open for Grandpa's truck. Once I see a truck that looks similar and my heart leaps into my mouth, but it's a young guy driving it with the radio up loud.

We stop at a grocery store and pick out some day-old bagels and candy bars for our lunch later on. I feel hyper-self-conscious in the store, like everyone knows I'm some sort of runaway. After we pay, we walk back to the car and get in. I take a deep breath and head for the first stop on the river where Grandpa might be.

The river is crowded near the town, and Stink and I get out a few times and stand on the bank to get a better look at the fishermen. I'd planned on just looking for Grandpa's truck parked along the side, but it made me nervous to depend only on that.

I get up my courage and talk to a man and woman getting their gear out of the back of their car.

"Have you seen an older man, with a bamboo rod, fishing anywhere along here?" I ask.

"No," says the man. "We just got in this morning."

The woman smiles at me. "Are you lost?"

"No, just looking for my grandpa," I say.

"Is he lost?" The woman looks concerned.

"He ran away," volunteers Stink. "We're going to find him and bring him home."

"Shouldn't you call the police?" The woman isn't smiling anymore.

"He's just fishing," I say. "We got our wires crossed about the location. Thanks for your help."

I grab Stink's ear and hustle him back to the car.

"What?" he says. "Ow!"

I let go.

"You can't be telling people that," I say.

"It's the truth!"

"I know, but don't you get it? We could get in trouble. Grandpa's an adult. We are kids—minors," I say. "To anyone else, we're runaways. Mom may even have the police looking for us."

Stink's eyes get wide. "Why would she do that? Will they put us in jail?"

"No, they won't put us in jail. They'd probably just send us back home," I say. Stink doesn't seem comforted.

"But you're the only one who knows where to find Grandpa," he says. "No one else is doing anything."

"That's right. And that's why you can't be saying stuff that will make anyone suspicious. Let me do the talking. Got it?"

"Got it," Stink says. "I'm the knucklehead."

We stop every place we see a car parked or a group of fishermen along the river. We don't get any real clues, but people are friendly, and I'm feeling hopeful.

After a few hours and a few false leads, I finally give in to Stink, who wants a break. We take our food out of the car and find a nice place by the river to eat, a flat spot with a big boulder for a table. The ground is dry in the sunny spots, which are few because the evergreens are thick and the other trees still have most of their leaves. Large black ants weave in and out of the twigs and pebbles on the ground and crawl up the rock around our food. The river is loud here, the water crashing into a pile of rocks and spilling down a three-foot drop. We sit close enough to the water so tiny droplets spray us when a breeze picks them up.

After lunch, Stink goes down by the river's edge and tosses rocks into the water. I lie down and rest, listening to the water rush by. I love the sound. It's predictable and permanent, that sound, even if the river itself is always changing.

"Will it ever run out?" I remember I'd asked Grandpa, the first time he'd taken me here to teach me how to cast the line from a fly rod into a real river. He'd taught me before, when I was barely old enough to understand, out in the backyard, but now it was time for the real thing.

"Not in our lifetime," Grandpa said. "Probably not in a million years."

"But where does all the water come from?" I imagined a big faucet somewhere, way up in the mountain.

"It's melted snow," he said.

"But why does it all come down right here? How come it doesn't just wash down the mountain any old way?" That was a neat image, the mountain as one big waterfall.

"It's predetermined," Grandpa said. "The water has to go the path of least resistance. That's why it's all together, here, in a path that the water has cut out for thousands of years."

That bothered me, that the melted snow had no choice how it wanted to get down the mountain. Predetermined. I didn't quite believe it. New paths could be cut, couldn't they?

I'd cast my line over and over into the river that day, into the deep, shaded pools and behind big boulders where the trout were holding, but I never did get a bite. Grandpa pulled out fish after fish. It didn't matter. I was more interested in the water.

I'm half-asleep when big drops of icy water hit my face. I suck in air and sit straight up. Stink's standing there, dripping wet clear up to his waist.

"What the . . ."

"I got wet," he says. "I'm cold."

I have to take him to a fast-food joint so that he can change his clothes in the bathroom. The clothes he'd stashed in the trunk don't quite match, but they are good enough. Then he wants french fries, so I buy him a small package. By the time we get going again, it's almost two-thirty, and I'm frustrated. We drive around until it starts to get dark and we're not making any progress. It's been an extraordinarily long day. Hours have been added somehow, I'm sure, and yet I haven't made good use of them. I'm no closer to finding Grandpa than I was this morning.

We drive back into town and I decide our best bet at this point is to walk around, looking for Grandpa's truck. Mostly, I'm just cross and frustrated and I figure the walking will do me good. Besides, it's been so cold at night, it's possible he's staying in town. We don't stop for dinner, except to buy a few Powerbars that we eat while we're walking, which Stink whines about.

About ten-thirty, Stink starts to complain that his legs hurt.

"Why can't we drive the car?" he asks. "What are we looking for anyway?"

"We don't want to waste gas," I tell him. "And we're looking for Grandpa, stupid."

Stink looks mad, and I figure it's because I called him stupid. But after a minute, he says, "This was your big plan to find Grandpa? To walk around town looking for his truck?"

I'm instantly furious.

"No, this was not my big plan," I yell at him. A couple walking by looks at me, but I don't care. They don't look much older than me. I continue yelling. "Plans don't always work. This is not my fault!" The couple stops to listen. They pretend they're reading a poster in a store window. "Grandpa didn't have to leave!" I'm too upset to stop, but in a lower voice, I say, "I'm just trying to make things better. No one asked you to come with me! You don't have anything to do with this anyway!"

Both the girl and the boy are now blatantly staring. "What are you staring at?" I holler at them. They look at each other, then the girl pulls on the boy's arm and they go away, laughing.

I expect Stink to start crying, and when he doesn't, it surprises me. He looks me square in the eyes and then does his own yelling.

"This has as much to do with me as anything else. Mom never pays attention to me. I'll bet she wishes I was never born." He rubs at his nose. "Anyway, it's like my dad never existed. It's Jack this and Jack that and wasn't Jack wonderful. I'm not even related to Grandma, or Grandpa, and I'm only half-related to you, by a mom who doesn't give a crap!" I expect him to break out in some Three Stooges act, but he's still serious. "You're all I've got, Callie! You're all I've got!" His eyes waver from my face and he does start to cry. "You're all I've got, and you wish I would go away, too, just like everyone else. Well, I'm not going away, because there's nowhere for me to go."

I'm completely stunned at the truth of Stink's outburst. I don't know what to say.

"I didn't want to be without you. I would have been scared," Stink says, his voice soft and broken by crying.

"Don't worry," I say. I put my arm across his skinny shoulders and it hangs there awkwardly, but there's nothing else I can think to do. "Don't worry," I say again, but now I'm worried sick.

It's true that Stink has been an afterthought to Mom. I've been pretty much taking care of him since he was two or three. I wonder if this is not so much because she started neglecting him but because I took over. She used to let him go out and play near the street. I was terrified he'd go out too far and get hit by a car, so I started watching him. She also used to feed him Kool-Aid all day long, and I'd dump it out and fill his cup with milk instead.

I buy Stink some ice cream at a parlor, even though it's cold outside. As he's sitting at the table, I count the money we have left. Fifty-two dollars. I take out Mom's credit card and rub it on my pants, praying it's the magnetic strip that's gone bad and not her credit.

We find a room at a place that's forty-two dollars a night. I hand the woman at the counter the credit card.

"Where's your mom or dad?" she asks, right off.

"Uh, they're going to be out real late, so they sent me ahead to check in, so me and my brother could get some sleep," I say. Pretty good, I think.

"Well, it isn't what we usually do . . . ," the woman says.

"We're really tired," I say. "My mom gave me the credit card. She said if there were any problems, she'd come in later."

The woman shrugs her shoulders and turns around. I breathe easier.

"This card's been rejected," she says when she comes back from the little room behind the counter.

"It's probably just the magnetic strip. My mom uses it so often, it's a little worn out. Try punching in the numbers." I try to stay calm, and act like this is no big deal.

"Okay, I'll try," the woman says. Thank goodness she's nice enough.

She comes out with the credit card in her outstretched hand.

"Didn't work, either," she says.

"Probably just a bank error," I say. I look down at my shoes and consider what to do. Sleep in the car? No, we'd freeze. There's not enough gas to keep it running, and there're no blankets. Why didn't I bring blankets? Drive back to Grandma's without Grandpa. We'd be back by two in the morning. It would probably be the best thing for Stink. But I couldn't face Mom or Grandma, and I'm so tired I'm afraid to drive.

"We'll pay cash," I tell the woman. I dig out the money and hand it to her. She looks at me like she's not sure she ought to trust me, but checks us in.

It doesn't occur to me until we are settled down for the night that I haven't left enough money for gas to get home. There's about an eighth of a tank left, and it takes one and a half tanks to get to Grandma's from here.

I'm so exhausted I don't have the energy to get upset, but I can't sleep, as usual. I think about Raf, instead, and how much I miss him. I want to talk to him. I want to hear his voice. I want to ask him what I should do. I shouldn't waste money for even a phone call. Is this what being in love is? Or do I just need Raf? I remember what Stink said earlier, and I know that he needs me. There's nobody else for him. I can't afford to love Raf, because I don't have anything to give back. My family has run me dry.

But I do call Raf from the pay phone outside, at three in the morning. He answers the phone, sounds wide awake, like he's been waiting for me.

"It's me," I say.

"I know," Raf says. I want to cry at the sound of his voice.

"Callie, come back. Please come back," he says.

"No," I say. "One more day. I need another day."

"Then let me come be with you. I don't know how to help, but let me be there for you," he says. His voice sinks right into my heart and my chest feels like it's going to explode.

I hear someone talking in the background at Raf's house.

"Just a minute," he says, and I think he puts his hand over the phone, but I can still hear.

"It's for me," he says, really annoyed at whoever it is.

"Who's calling at this hour?" Raf's mom.

"Never mind," Raf says. "Go back to bed." Why does he treat her like that? Maybe he's trying to protect me. Maybe he doesn't want her to know that I would be so rude as to call at this hour. I hope that's it, because I can't stand the thought that Raf would take a mother like that for granted. They argue some more, and then Raf comes back on the line.

"I'm so sorry," I say.

"For what?"

For loving you, I think. You don't know what you're getting into, I think.

"For getting you involved in this," I say.

"I'm not involved in this, I'm involved with you," he says.

"I'm sorry," I say again.

"Listen to you. No one's twisting my arm, Callie. Please let me come help you."

"Your parents wouldn't let you," I say.

"That doesn't matter," he says.

"It does," I say, and think, you have no idea, Raf. "I just need one more day and I'll be back."

Raf's quiet for a long time. "Are you sure you're okay?"

"Yeah, I'm sure," I tell him. "Good night, Raf."

"Good night, Callie. Take care of yourself. I'll see you tomorrow?"

"See you tomorrow," I say, and pray it's not a lie.

chapter eleven

When I wake up, it takes me a minute to remember I am in a motel, in West Yellowstone, alone with Stink, and that I have to find Grandpa. I open my eyes and think about our last ten dollars. My head swims, my chest feels heavy, and blackness closes in from both sides until I have no peripheral vision. I could drown in the blackness; it would be easier than finding the strength to get out of bed.

The heavy dark curtains that cover the ground-level window of our room make it impossible to tell if it is morning. But I hear footsteps from the room above ours and a shower running somewhere, so it must be.

"Callie?"

I take a deep breath and close my eyes again.

"Callie? Something's wrong with me."

I roll over and look at Stink. He sits on the edge of the couch, scratching his chest.

"I itch," he says. He sounds frightened. He scratches harder.

My vision is still blurry and the light is not good, but I see spots on Stink's face.

"I think I have a fever."

"Come here," I say, throwing the covers aside.

Stink walks over and flips on the bedside lamp.

"Ouch!" he says when I grab the hair on top of his head to tilt his face up toward mine, so that I can get a closer look.

"You've got spots! All over!" I say. "What on earth . . ."

"Chicken pox has been going around at school," Stink offers. "But I didn't think I'd get it because it's been two weeks. . . ."

"Chicken pox. You've got chicken pox!" I tell him.

Stink's eyes get round and he starts to cry. I get angry.

"This is perfect. Just fine and dandy. Now what am I supposed to do?"

"I don't know," he blubbers. "I didn't get them on purpose."

I practice Dad's breathing exercises.

"No, no, of course you didn't get chicken pox on purpose," I say. "But what am I supposed to do?" I shout this last part. So much for the breathing. Stink crawls back under the blanket on the couch and itches and cries. I remember when he was three and came down with a nasty flu. I used to get up at night and sneak into his room and peek at him to make sure he was okay and bring him a drink of water if he was awake. I'd sing to him and he'd suck his thumb and go back to sleep. Back then I never got angry.

I try and make myself remember our conversation last night. I try and make myself have compassion for Stink. But it ends up I don't have to try too hard. I'm angry at myself, for being responsible for this mess. I'd be better off if I didn't care how Stink felt.

Think. I've got to think. I can't turn around and go back without Grandpa. I couldn't even if I wanted to. Ten dollars of gas wouldn't get us halfway there, and there is no way I can show up and face my mother and Grandma without Grandpa. We need money, I haven't found Grandpa, Stink is a mess, and we need money. How can I get some money?

While I'm stressing about this, Stink's crying and scratching gets to me and I feel bad for him. Annoyed, too, but not as much as I normally would be. I put on my coat and shoes.

"I'll be right back."

"Where are you going?" Stink asks.

"Just hang tight," I tell him. "I'm going to get you something to help you stop itching."

I forget about using up gas and I go to a market that's open early. I buy baking soda and oatmeal, because I can't remember which you're supposed to add to a bath to stop itching. And I buy a cheap, generic brand of Benadryl, because I think it's supposed to work, too. I spend six dollars and forty-eight cents.

When I get back to the motel, I fill up the bathtub and dump in both the baking soda and oatmeal. It looks disgusting.

"I'm not getting in that," Stink says, wrinkles his nose, and scratches.

"Oh, yes, you are," I tell him. "And take a swig of this." I hand him the open bottle of medicine and he takes a tiny sip. "A little more," I tell him. "You need at least a tablespoon. Okay, now into the tub you go. I've got to go do some things. You stay here. Don't go any-where until I get back. I'm going to see if you can stay a little past checkout time, so don't wander off."

Stink looks at me like I'm nuts, but he heads to the tub without another word.

I make sure the door is locked behind me and go to the motel office.

"Excuse me." I'm relieved it's the same nice woman who was there last night.

"Yes?"

"My little brother is not feeling well, and I've got to

run some errands before we can check out. Can he stay until noon? That is, if it isn't too much trouble."

"Where are your parents?" she asks.

Shoot. Why didn't I think through a lie before I started?

"They got up real early and left before they knew he wasn't feeling good. We're supposed to meet them in town later." I'm getting good at lying.

She types into the computer on the desk and looks up at me. "Yes, but only until noon. We're almost full up, but most won't check in until later. And we need time to clean."

"Thank you. Thanks, I really mean it. I'll hurry," I say, rushing out before she asks any more questions.

chapter twelve

I drive to a spot on the river where there are a lot of
trucks parked. There are four or five groups of fishermen, mostly middle-aged men. No women. I was hoping there would be some women. But I can tell from the
way most of the men are wearing new-looking gear
from Orvis that they are beginners. Real pros look a
little banged up and don't go for the stuff in the glossy
catalogs. I open the trunk of the car and take out
Grandpa's tackle box. I take a deep breath and open the
door.

I approach a young guy first, who has a baseball cap
pulled low over his forehead. He's sitting on a stump,
away from all the others, struggling to tie a fly onto his
leader. He looks up at me, out from under his cap.

"Howdy," he says.

"Hi." My voice comes out a squeak. I clear my
throat and try again.

"I've got some flies here that are top quality, hand-made," I say. "You can't find any better."

He leans forward.

"You do, do you?" He spins his cap around back-ward. He's got long dusty brown lashes, and clear blue eyes, but they're a little bit squinty. "Let's have a look-see."

I drop Grandpa's box in front of him and open it.

The guy picks up a few flies and turns them over and over. "Very nice, very nice," he keeps saying. He turns and opens his own tiny fly box with store-bought flies. None of them is exactly right for this hatch, but he obviously doesn't know it.

"These flies will work better than anything you've got there," I tell him.

"Oh yeah?" he says, studying my face with those light-colored eyes. I'm getting uneasy, but I can't say why, exactly. Something about the way he's looking at me.

"I'll sell them cheap," I say.

"Sell them?" He's surprised. What did he think I was doing? Showing off?

"Well, yes," I say. "I need some money." I know I shouldn't have said that the minute it comes out of my mouth.

"What's your name?" he asks. He's smiling, making his eyes narrow even more. I notice the wrinkles around them. He's older than I first thought.

"Callie," I say, and immediately think I should have made something up. At least I didn't give my last name. I need to be more careful. My palms start to sweat when I realize most of the other people have moved farther away, out of earshot.

"Well, Callie . . ." The way he says my name makes my cheeks burn and I want to leave. "Where did you get these? How old are you?"

"Eighteen," I lie. "I tied these flies. With my grandpa."

He looks at me hard, with a slight frown on his face. Like he can see clear through me. I try to keep my face pleasant-looking. Finally, he digs out a five-dollar bill.

"Give me a couple of those," he says, and points to some small brown ones.

"Good choice," I say. My hand is shaking a little as I pick the flies out of the container and hand them over. He gives me the money and I turn to go.

"Hey!"

I turn my head to look back, but I don't stop. I want to run.

"Thanks," he says, and smiles a little.

My heart stops beating so fast and I wonder why I'm so freaked out. That was easy enough. But still, I get in the car and drive away. I want to find a new spot. That guy has my skin all crawly, the way he looked at me like that. I think I'm getting a little paranoid. I drive up by the river, around a loop, and back up the road again, and that's when I see Grandpa's pickup. I'm halfway past it. I slam on the brakes. The car behind me squeals to a stop, then sheds rubber going around me. The driver, a girl, gives me the finger but I don't care. I back up in the middle of the road and pull in next to Grandpa's truck. I hop out. The doors of the pickup are locked, but I can see his things inside. *Thank you thank you thank you* I say over and over to no one in particular.

I start down the trail that leads to the river and I hear a commotion.

"I ain't jumped no one's hole!" It's Grandpa, I think, but he sounds different. Maybe it's not. Some mumbling, and then I know it is Grandpa. He's been drinking.

"I said I ain't jumped no one's hole!" His words are slurred and slow. "I'm a gentleman fisherman. Ain't jumped no one's hole ever and I been fishin' this river before any of you stopped pissin' in your pants and callin' fer yer mammy!"

There's a bunch of other voices, but none loud like Grandpa's.

A man with a cell phone passes me on the trail. I can tell he's a fishing guide by the way he's got a pack up around his chest and a lanyard with tools around his neck.

92

"Yeah, we got a live one down here on the riverbank at about milepost thirty-seven, right around the bend."

Who's he talking to? The police? The man keeps walking and talking.

"No, no weapons or fighting. He threw a punch. But he's an old man. Falling-down drunk. Okay, yeah, thanks." He clicks off his phone and turns around.

"Cops are coming!" he yells down the trail.

I'm close enough now to see two men in thick waders. Their backs are to me, and they're talking to each other, real low. I move up behind them, close.

Then Grandpa is there, right in one of their faces.

"Did ya hear what I was sayin'?" I can see the spit fly.

"We heard you, mister," the man says. "We aren't messing with you. You haven't jumped our hole. You are absolutely right."

"That's right," Grandpa slurs. The men turn around and see me standing there.

"You better go away, girl," one says as they walk by. "The cops are coming for this drunk."

"Callie!" Grandpa staggers up to me. Both men put themselves back between Grandpa and me. "What a nice surprise!"

"Go back up the trail," one says. "We'll deal with him. Hurry, please." The men don't look brave at all. In fact, I can tell they're afraid of Grandpa.

"It's okay," I tell them. "He's my grandpa. I've come to take him home."

"We ain't goin' home, Callie! The fishin's been great." He's pushed through the men and I can smell the liquor on him. "Come fish with me, here. Just like when you was little."

One of the men grabs Grandpa's arm, to protect me, I guess. Grandpa swings around and hits him square in the nose. The man swears and puts his hands to his face. Blood gushes out between his fingers. I don't wait any longer.

"We've got to get out of here, Grandpa," I say, grabbing his hand. It's like he's glued to the ground.

"Is Rachel missing me?" Grandpa says. "I done her wrong again. I need to 'pologize."

Please, please, please. I pull hard on his arm. He comes with me willingly then, but stares back at the man holding his face. The other guy looks at me and at his friend, like he doesn't know who needs him more. I rush Grandpa up the trail and practically shove him into the car, while the guide stares at us. Grandpa's a big man, but he's unsteady and I'm not afraid of him. "It's okay," I shout to the guide. "I'll take care of him. Sorry about the trouble."

"I've got my truck," he says, once we're in the car. "But I parked 'er over there last night 'cause I had a little whiskey." He points an unsteady finger.

"That's okay, Grandpa," I say. "We'll come back later."

As I race into town, we pass the cop who's on his way to get Grandpa. I hope the men don't send the cops after us. I slow down. The last thing I need is to be pulled over for speeding.

We get to the motel, and Grandpa's asleep or passed out. Either way, I'm relieved. But now I'm worried about Stink. I should have measured out the medicine. What if he's fallen asleep in the tub? I try to be calm, and head to the office first, to tell the lady we'd hurry up and clear out of the room.

"No need," she says. "Some boy came and paid cash for another day. So you're good till tomorrow morning."

"Who was it?" I ask.

"Some boy, like I said. Didn't give his name. Real cute, but young-looking. Where'd you say your parents were?"

I'm already halfway out the door, running to our room. The door's not locked and I fling it open. Raf and Stink are sitting on the bed, playing cards. Stink's covered in angry red spots but he's smiling wide.

"Look who's here!" he shouts, even though I'm standing two feet away.

"Look who's here," I repeat, stunned.

Raf stands up and meets me halfway in a hug.

"What are you doing here?" I say into his neck. "How did you find us?"

He pulls away from me and looks into my eyes. His beautiful, dark eyes. I look down, embarrassed.

"I've got Caller ID," he says.

"Yeah, Mrs. Wizard!" Stink shouts. "He rode his dirt bike the whole way!"

"I'm glad you're here," I say, ignoring Stink, but I don't necessarily mean it. I'm uneasy that he's come this far, for me.

"I came to help you find your grandpa," Raf says. "I'll catch heck, but as long as I'm back before tomorrow night . . . It doesn't matter. I don't care what Mom thinks."

Raf, you should care, I think, and be grateful. I have a weird feeling in my stomach. Raf seems like a stranger, somehow, now that he's here in the middle of all this.

"Grandpa's in the car," I say.

"Yahoo!" Stink shouts, and starts to run to the door.

"Not so fast." I grab him by the back of his shirt. "He's drunk."

"Oh." Stink sits back down on the bed and scratches.

"He needs to sober up before we can go home."

Raf says, "Let's get him out of the car and into a bed."

Raf and I go out and rouse Grandpa. He keeps his eyes shut, but he does help us by putting some weight on his own legs. We walk him around back, so the motel lady won't see. By the time we've gotten his shoes off and him into the bed, Raf and I are breathing hard and sweaty, and I'm a little sick from the smell of the alcohol coming off Grandpa.

"I didn't know he was a drinker," Raf says, wiping his forehead.

"He's not," I say. "I mean, not normally. Just once in a while. But when he does drink, he tends to overdo it."

"That's an understatement," Raf says. "Do you want me to call your mom and Rachel? They ought to know."

I hadn't thought about this. I'd imagined myself driving home with Grandpa to hugs and smiles and everyone happy because I'd reunited the family.

"I guess so," I say, then, "I better do it."

Raf retrieves a bunch of quarters from his pocket and hands them to me. "You did it, Callie," he says.

I smile and walk out the door. Did what? Caused a lot of trouble, I guess, but at least Grandpa's in the motel bed, snoring away, safe. Mrs. Carmona's not going to like me so much anymore. I didn't ask for Raf's help. Did I wish for it?

I dial Grandma's number.

"Hello?" It's Mom.

"I've got Grandpa," I say.

"Callie? Where in the devil . . ."

"Mom, listen to me. I'm sorry if you've been worried. But I found Grandpa."

"Where is he?" she asks. "Is he okay?"

I'm okay, I think, thanks for asking. "He's been drinking. I've got him sleeping in a motel room right now. We'll bring him home when he's ready."

"Well." Mom takes a deep breath. "I don't know what to say. You don't realize the hell you've put me through."

"I'm sorry. I didn't mean to put you through anything. I just wanted to fix things."

"Callie Lucinda Gray, there are some things you can't fix. I have half a mind to—"

"To what, Mom?" To what? I've been my own person for years. What could she do, what could she say that would make any difference at all?

"Just come home. You and Ronnie and Grandpa. Just come home."

"We'll be back tomorrow, Mom. I promise." I hang up. You're welcome, I think. You're welcome and I love you, too. I want to punch my fist through the brick wall of the motel. Instead I kick a rock hard into the parking lot. I concentrate on the fact that I've found Grandpa and that Raf is here, and I need to deal with Stink and his chicken pox.

Grandpa snores all day, stirring only a few times. Raf goes on his dirt bike to retrieve Grandpa's truck. I'm worried he'll get a ticket for riding his dirt bike on the roads, but he doesn't listen to me. I offer to drive him to get it, but he says I shouldn't leave Grandpa and Stink alone, and anyway, he's just going to throw the dirt bike in the back of the truck and come back. It makes me a little upset that he's doing so much, but when he gets back I breathe easier. Raf, Stink, and I play cards and order in pizza, which Raf pays for.

Stink tells Raf all his Three Stooges stories and Raf doesn't seem to mind. I'm grateful, because it gives me time to think.

"Did you know in one episode," Stink says, "the Stooges are floating down the street on a mattress and if you look in the windows of the shops behind them, you can see a guy with a hose squirting the street?"

Raf laughs and looks at me.

"How does he know these things?" he asks.

"Years of practice," I say. "At least he doesn't act them out anymore. You should have been there when he poured airplane glue on Grandpa's chair, or when he hid in the cabbages at the grocery store." It's suddenly easy, the three of us being together, and I try to relax a little.

"Raf, are you going to be in big trouble?" I ask.

"Yeah," he says. "But it's okay. Mom's overprotective. I can't be like she wants me to be all the time. I'm not as good as you, Callie." I close my eyes and pretend to nap because I'm uncomfortable again at how much Raf has helped me.

At about eight o'clock, we're watching a dumb sit-com on TV and Grandpa sits up in bed and rubs his head.

"Grandpa? How are you feeling?" I walk over and sit next to him. "Are you okay?"

He looks at the back of his hand and turns it over and over. "Did I really punch that guy in the face?" he asks.

"Yeah, you really did," I say.

"My hand hurts." He presses each knuckle with the thumb of the other hand.

"Grandpa, why?"

"Don't know," he says, and gets up to use the bathroom. He's steady on his feet.

When he comes back, Stink walks over and gives him a hug.

"I thought I'd sobered up, but I'm seeing spots," Grandpa says.

"Chicken pox," Stink says. Scratch, scratch. "I'm glad we found you."

"Didn't know I was lost," he says.

The door shuts and Raf is gone. What's he doing now?

"Grandpa, why did you leave?" I ask. "Why did you

leave Grandma and the farm and right before the auction . . . Don't you know how sick with worry we've been? How could you?" I feel like I should be feeling angry, but I'm only sad.

Grandpa sighs and rubs at his temples.

"Well, I needed a break," he says. "I just needed a fishing trip. To clear my mind. That's all. Didn't want to tell anyone where I was going because there hasn't been anything but weepin' and naggin' back at the farm. I did the best I could. Just thought I needed a break. Not easy, selling the farm, you know." He stops rubbing his head and looks up at me. "How did you find me?"

"You said before you died, you wanted to catch the Baetis hatch on the Gallatin River. You took your bamboo rod and blue-winged olives. Lucky guess."

"You always were a smart kid, Callie. But I ain't planning on dying any time soon." He smiles and then says, "You're smarter than your dad ever was."

"My dad the genius?"

"Genius," Grandpa says, and laughs a little. "Coward is more like it."

"What do you mean, a coward?"

He's rubbing at his temples again, leaving big red marks.

The door opens and Raf walks in with three Cokes and a Styrofoam cup. He hands the cup to Grandpa.

"It's hot," he says. Coffee. Grandpa sips at it without saying thanks. Raf hands one Coke to me and one to Stink.

"Thanks," I say. I turn back to Grandpa. I want him to explain what he meant about my dad being a coward.

But he changes the subject. "How's your mom doing?"

"The same," I say. "Still working a lot, can't focus on anything at home, doesn't care two cents about me or Stink." I'm still smarting from our phone conversation.

"Does she get out much? Have a boyfriend?" he asks.

"No, no. Nothing like that. Not since Stan. She says she'll never get over my dad," I say. I think of her sitting nights, staring out the window.

"She needs to put him to rest," Grandpa says. "Rachel, too. Neither one has been the same since."

"I can't remember what she was like before," I say. Mom has had a hole in her heart for so long. "If she cared enough about me, and about Stink, she'd get up and do something."

I've tapped into a deep well of anger inside myself. "In fact, I'm considering moving out of the house. She doesn't want me, doesn't need me. I'll do fine on my own. I've proven that the last few days." I'm shocked I've said this, but I don't take it back.

"You don't know what you're talking about,"

Grandpa says. "Your mom needs you as much as anyone on the face of the earth could need another person."

"She has a funny way of showing it," I say. My eyes are brimming with hot, angry tears. "We all had a loss, not just her."

Grandpa cringes when I say this, and then starts pacing the room. "A damn fool coward, Jack was. Taking off across Montana like he did, and leaving you and your mother behind. You weren't nothin' but a baby."

"I was five, and so what's wrong with a little vacation? He wasn't leaving us forever, just a few weeks. And at least *he* told us where he was going!" The tears flood over and burn my cheeks. "At least he told us where he was going." I say this last part again to hurt Grandpa, and it works.

"Callie, you need to know Jack had no intention of coming back," Grandpa says. "I was just goin' fishin' to clear my head. I never would have done a foolhardy cowardly thing like Jack did."

Raf says, "Come on, Ronnie, let's go play the video games in the lobby," and takes Stink by the arm.

"But I don't have my shoes . . . ," Stink protests. Raf practically shoves him out the door.

"What thing did he do?"

"Crossing Montana, then killing himself. Didn't leave a note, never called, nothing. Just left your mom to pick up the pieces."

Grandpa's words feel like a two-by-four swung right into my stomach.

"B-b-but it was an accident. . . . He hit the sign, and h-he was probably going too fast . . ." I manage. As I stutter these words, I know what I've believed all along isn't true. Maybe I've even felt it wasn't true, but wouldn't let myself think he could leave me on purpose.

"My hell, that sign wouldn't have killed a bird. Flimsy thing. Took an overdose of drugs, enough to kill an army, and went out on the road, knowing full well what he was doing. Lucky he didn't kill somebody else, driving full of drugs, and end up a murderer, too."

I want to think Grandpa's still drunk, not right in the head. But his words are steady and he's standing on his feet, his own old self. And my own head feels light, like I've let go of something heavy and dropped it into my heart instead.

"Callie, your mom feels responsible, you know. They had a big fight right before he left on his trip. Over their money troubles, over him not keeping a job. She told him she didn't care if he ever came back. And he didn't." Grandpa stops pacing and looks me square in the eyes.

"They fought all the time, though," I say. "He must have known she didn't really mean it. Why would he do something like that?"

"Damn coward," Grandpa says.

But I know that isn't it. As angry as I want to be now, at Dad, I'm not, because it's as if a missing puzzle piece has dropped from the sky. I think of the breathing exercises, the days he spent shut in his room. Out of work, responsible for me, but I ate lunch out of cereal boxes. His big ideas, how we always needed money, how he never lasted at a job. The breathing exercises. All the memories are a confusing flood, but they make sense in their own way, in the finality of what my dad did.

"You ain't like that, Callie, and neither am I. I may have left, but I'm going back. Always had every intention to. You may not think much of me right now, but I own up to my responsibilities, and so do you. You and me ain't like Jack at all." He's looking right into me. But I know he's not seeing. How much I am like Dad. The breathing exercises, the blackness.

"Why didn't Mom or Grandma, or you, ever tell me?" I ask. My voice doesn't sound like my own.

Grandpa fishes a piece of gum from his shirt pocket. He's never without gum since he stopped smoking.

"This family ain't exactly known for the ability to face things the way they are," he says. "It's easier for them to think Jack was some sort of genius who got in a tragic accident. They know the truth, just don't want to face it. Like I said, your mom feels responsible."

He must see the growing anger on my face, because he continues, "I'm sure they wanted to protect you, too. It ain't a tidy thing to know your own dad done something like that to himself." He cracks his gum. "As for me, I was told, in so many words, to stay the hell out of it. You were too little to understand, anyway."

Grandpa sits down on the bed. "My head hurts."

Mine, too.

"I need to go home and make this up to Rachel," he says wearily.

I go get Raf and Stink from the lobby. It's amazing to me that I can still walk and function and act normal.

Grandpa's ready to go, and I tell Stink to go home with him because I need a little more time to think.

"*Soitenly,*" Stink says, and hugs me tight around the waist.

Grandpa doesn't say anything about me not being old enough to drive, but he presses fifty bucks into my hand.

"You going with them, Raf?" I ask.

"No, I'll just leave the bike in the back of the truck. I'm not leaving you here alone," he says. I can feel blood rising in my face because Raf is being so difficult by being so good.

"It's okay," I say. "I'm just going to rest awhile. You don't need to worry about me."

"I want to stay with you."

"But I'm not leaving until tomorrow morning. There's something I need to do first."

"Anything, Callie," Raf says. He pulls me close and kisses my forehead. And then I cry.

chapter thirteen

At first, after Grandpa and Stink leave, it's odd to be alone in a motel room with Raf. Raf feels it, too, and we watch more TV, sitting up straight and keeping a little distance. Only our hands touch. I am glad he's stayed, after all. Now that Grandpa and Stink are gone, and after what I've been told about Dad, I'm feeling unsure about wanting to be alone. But I can tell he's feeling bad about something because he's quiet and doesn't look at me much. Maybe he's worried about the trouble he's in. Maybe I'm too much trouble. Maybe I haven't been grateful enough.

After the latest late show, I'm finally so exhausted I crawl into bed with my clothes on. Raf turns off the light and lies down on the couch.

"Come sleep in the bed," I tell Raf. I want to be close to him. The awkwardness of having him here has worn off. "That couch is infested with chicken pox germs."

I expect him to say no, but he comes right over and gets under the covers with me. He wraps his arms around me and brushes the hair out of my eyes. He still seems a little stiff, but I can tell he's trying to relax. He lifts my chin so we're looking into each other's eyes, I think, but it's awfully dark.

He kisses me lightly. Now I'm not nervous at all. I kiss him, hard, and get myself as close to him as I can. He pulls away from me quickly.

"Callie, you know how much I like you. In fact, I think I'm falling in love with you," he says. "But you need some sleep. It's been a hard day for everyone. I'm going to sleep right here next to you, so you won't feel alone, but you know you can trust me, right?" This last part sounds rehearsed.

"Yeah, I know," I say. Raf is so frustratingly good. What a nice way of telling me to back off. I consider feeling embarrassed, or offended. Or maybe Raf doesn't like me as much as I think. But he's here, isn't he? And didn't he just say he's falling in love with me? I kiss him again, and he doesn't push me away, but he does keep his distance, and holds my hands tight in his.

I'm so confused, so exhausted, so drained, I'm suddenly grateful for whatever it is in him that keeps my life from getting more complicated.

I don't sleep very well, but I like Raf sleeping next to me. I put my hand on his chest, lightly, so that I can feel him breathing. I stay that way for what seems like hours. I let myself think about Mom's pain and imagine her sitting at the window, night after night, looking out into the rain and wondering how things could have been different. And feeling responsible. Responsible for the mess Dad made for all of us. When it starts to get light outside, just barely, I finally float into some dreams.

chapter fourteen

I wake up and remember that my dad killed himself. I'm paralyzed. The blackness that usually stays on the periphery closes in and I shut my eyes against it.

I don't know how long I stay there; time has a way of slowing down and sinking in when I feel this way. I hear the shower in the bathroom, and I swim to the surface of the darkness when I remember it's Raf, and that he's falling in love with me. I squeeze my eyes shut tight and try to get rid of the old uncomfortable feeling of not wanting Raf to help me so much. I try to focus on how I felt sleeping next to him last night.

When I get enough energy, I turn my head and look at the clock. Nine. I'll bet the library opens at ten. I sit up and get my balance for a minute.

Raf emerges from the bathroom, in clean jeans, a navy T-shirt, and dripping-wet hair. He takes my breath away until I realize that I've just rolled out of bed and must look like something the cat dragged in. That's what my dad used to say when he was up before me on a good day, making seaweed and tofu soup for me in the kitchen.

"Look what the cat dragged in," he would say.

"We don't have a cat," I remember answering. "It's me, Daddy, it's me!"

"Well, what do you know," he would say, scooping me up in his arms and tickling me. "It's Callie! My very own little girl!"

I put my hand up to my hair and try to smooth it out. My mouth tastes horrible. I didn't brush my teeth last night. Raf sits next to me on the bed and I wonder if I smell bad, too.

"Good morning," he says.

"Good morning," I mumble, with my hand over my mouth. "I need a shower." I stand up quickly and head to the bathroom.

"Wait a minute," Raf says. I turn and expect him to lie and say something like how beautiful I am in the morning.

"There's no hot water," he says. "I used it all up. Quality hotel."

"Great, thanks a lot," I say. It's hard to believe we're having this conversation. Like we've been together for years.

The cold water doesn't feel as bad as I thought it would. I guess when your body is bruised on the inside, nothing on the outside makes much difference. When I start to turn blue, I get out of the shower and put on my other set of clothes, which are wrinkled and not exactly clean. I'd expected to be here by myself, and not for nearly so long. I wet my hands and try to smooth out some of the wrinkles. I brush my teeth twice.

"Callie! Breakfast!" Raf calls out.

He's got croissants and hot chocolate and oranges. He's already cutting up the oranges with his pocket knife. I could get used to living with Raf, except for the hot water thing.

After we've eaten, and I've added a few new stains to my clothes from the juicy oranges, Raf says he needs to go use the phone to call his mom.

"You're going to be in big trouble, aren't you?" I ask.

"You keep asking me that. Yes, I'm in trouble. When I called Mom last night and told her I wouldn't be home until today, it didn't go over real big. I told her I was helping you with a family emergency."

"That's the truth," I say. "I'm sorry I've gotten you in trouble."

He shrugs his shoulders. "It was worth it. But whatever you do, don't tell my mother I stayed here in the same room with you last night."

"It's the least I can do," I say. "It's not like there's anything to hide." Raf looks as if I'd slapped him.

"I hope you don't think I'm some sort of a geek," Raf says.

"I love everything about you," I say. "Geek or no." What I really want to say is thank you thank you thank you for being so good and for not complicating things more than they need to be and for being here with me and for falling in love with me.

When Raf goes out to call his mom, I pick up the room as best I can. Raf's mom has more influence over him than he would like to believe. I smile, because it's good even if he doesn't think so. I go to check out of the room. It's the same nice lady. Doesn't she ever sleep or get a break?

"Good luck to you," she says as I leave.

Raf drives and drops me off at the library, while he goes to fill up the gas tank and get some snacks for the trip home.

The librarian shows me how to use the microfiche machine and helps me find the *Montana Expositor* reel with the right date.

As I'm rolling the film through, to get to August 14, I get vertigo and a sick feeling in my stomach. But finally I'm there, and I see the original article, the one my mom has stored in the box in her room, the box with nothing else in it. I roll the film to the next day. On page two, I find the headline: SEATTLE MAN'S DEATH RULED SUICIDE. So there it is. I take a deep breath and read:

Fairview, Montana. A Seattle man who died yesterday after he crashed his car into a state road sign committed suicide, according to the state coroner's office. Jack Gray, age 32, had a lethal level of antidepressants and methamphetamine in his blood. The overdose of drugs was the cause of death. According to his father, Charles Gray, of Idaho Falls, Idaho, his son had a history of depression and had attempted suicide at least two times previously.

So it's been here all along, in black and white, no question about it. And I've been living in the gray area, without a clear view of anything. There are a few more paragraphs, but I don't read them, because this is enough. I ask the librarian if she can change a dollar for me so that I can make a copy. She doesn't have enough change for my dollar, but gives me what she has after I tell her it doesn't matter. I put the dime in the machine and a copy of the article spits out the side. It's barely legible, but it's real. I fold it carefully in half, thank the librarian, and wait on the front steps for Raf.

I intend to put this article in the box with the other article Mom keeps.

Raf pulls up in a little while, and walks over to me. "Hey, ready to go?"

I show him the piece of paper.

"I'm sorry," he says. "I'm really sorry."

"Everybody knew but me, huh?"

"Yeah, I guess so."

"Raf, will you go on a trip with me? Across Montana?"

"Why?" Raf looks as stunned as I feel.

"Just because I need to."

"Callie, do you have any idea how big the state of Montana is? How long it would take? What about your mother? What about me? Do you know how much trouble I'll be in?" His voice has an edge to it. He's mad. I can't blame him. It does sound stupid. But I want to go. I can make the money Grandpa gave me last, and I don't give two hoots what Mom thinks. I care what Raf's mom thinks, I really do, but I can't stop.

"Come with me," I say.

Raf looks at me and I can tell he's questioning my sanity.

"I've come this far for you, but I can't do what you're asking."

"Then I'll go alone," I say. "It's better if I'm alone, anyway, if I'm going to sort this out. Drive me to a rental car place. You take Mom's car home and I'll rent one."

"You can't," Raf says. He's not even trying to hide his frustration. "You have to be twenty-one. You don't even look sixteen or seventeen. I don't know how you've pulled it off this far."

"Well, I have pulled it off, and I'll do it again," I say. "Just drive me into town and I'll get something." I walk to the car and get in. Raf doesn't follow me. I roll down the window. "Are you coming?"

Raf walks quickly to the car, gets in, and slams his door shut. We drive north instead of into town, in silence. I have found Grandpa, I have taken care of Stink. I've taken care of our problems the best I can. It's time I do something for myself. I'm tired of worrying about everyone else.

"You don't know what you're doing," Raf finally says.

"Pull the car over," I say.

"What?"

"Pull the car over," I say again.

"There's nothing here," Raf says. "We're in a national forest!"

"Pull over." I think about Mom staring out the window every night. Raf's right. I don't know what I'm doing.

He pulls the car over onto the gravel shoulder. I get out and Raf swears. He turns off the engine. I feel bad for making him swear.

On both sides of the road, there's nothing but trees and I can hear the river, the sound of water rushing by. I cross the road to get closer to the river. I close my eyes and block everything out but that sound. There is a small breeze that feels good on my face and the smell of the pine trees fills my nose. I tilt my head back and look up at the sky. There are a lot of gray clouds, but there are also patches of blue sky. Patches of sky that look brighter and bluer than I've ever noticed.

I understand my dad's blackness, but I can also see these patches of bright blue sky. I think of Raf in the car, waiting for me, impossibly good Raf. I think of Stink, and his chicken pox, and Grandma and Grandpa. And Mom, and how she doesn't understand the blackness in Dad, or in me. And how she doesn't understand it wasn't her fault. And there is that box, in Mom's room, that's waiting for something else.

"You and me ain't like Jack," Grandpa said. But I am like Jack, and I wonder if I have the strength to fight what ran through him and me, to carve my own path. I wonder if I can make Mom understand she wasn't responsible, and get us all some help. Whatever it is that I have, that Jack had, is bigger than all of us. I stare at those patches of sky until they burn into my eyes and when I close my eyes they are still there.

I walk back to the car and get in.

"Let's go," I tell Raf.

He starts the car and keeps going north.

"Wait," I say. "I meant, let's go home."

"You sure, Callie?"

"I'm sure. Let's go back to Idaho."

He pulls a U-turn and drives fast. I reach over and touch his hand when we cross the border, leaving Montana behind.